FROM THE
NANCY DREW FILES

ASSIGNMENT: Find the practical joker who's stalking the Emerson College basketball team—before they blow their chance for the playoffs.

CONTACT: Coach Pat Burnett. When the campus police aren't helpful, he takes Ned's suggestion and asks Nancy to investigate.

SUSPECTS: Mike O'Shea—co-captain of the team and Ned's really good friend. Ned swears he's innocent. So why is there incriminating evidence in his room?

Ray Ungar—he was dropped from the team for bad grades. Now he's bitter. Would he sabotage the Wildcats for revenge?

Tom Stafford—student council president. He's on a crusade to get the athletics budget cut. How far is he willing to go—all the way to murder?

COMPLICATIONS: It was Ned's idea to get Nancy on the case, but he didn't plan on his best friend being her #1 suspect. How well does he really know the girl he loves? Now the joker's on to Nancy. It's not just the team that's in danger—Nancy and her friends are, too.

Books in THE NANCY DREW FILES® Series

Available from ARCHWAY paperbacks

THE NANCY DREW FILES™ CASE · 8

TWO POINTS TO MURDER

Carolyn Keene

AN ARCHWAY PAPERBACK
Published by POCKET BOOKS • NEW YORK

This novel is a work of fiction. Names, characters, places and incidents are either the product of the author's imagination or are used fictitiously. Any resemblance to actual events or locales or persons, living or dead, is entirely coincidental.

AN ARCHWAY PAPERBACK *Original*

 An Archway Paperback published by
POCKET BOOKS, a division of Simon & Schuster, Inc.
1230 Avenue of the Americas, New York, N.Y. 10020

Copyright © 1987 by Simon & Schuster, Inc.
Cover artwork copyright © 1987 Enric
Produced by Mega-Books of New York, Inc.

ISBN: 0-671-63079-2

First Archway Paperback printing February 1987

10 9 8 7 6 5 4 3 2

NANCY DREW, AN ARCHWAY PAPERBACK and colophon
are registered trademarks of Simon & Schuster, Inc.

THE NANCY DREW FILES is a trademark
of Simon & Schuster, Inc.

Printed in the U.S.A.

IL 7+

Acknowledgments

Special thanks to
Marvin Kaye and Irvin Muchnick
for their technical advice.

Chapter

One

GREAT, WE'RE ALMOST there," Nancy Drew announced, swinging her bright blue Mustang down the interstate's exit ramp.

In the backseat, Bess Marvin giggled in excitement. "All right! Emerson College, look out! Here we come!"

"You mean, look out, Emerson *boys,*" George Fayne teased, twisting around in the front passenger seat. "Admit it, Bess . . . you came along on this trip mostly to meet a lot of cute undergraduate guys, right?"

"Wrong!" Bess gave her shiny, straw-blond hair an indignant toss. "How come you always assume

1

I've got boys on the brain? The truth is, I came along to help Nancy with her case."

"Yeah, right," George drawled.

"I mean it! If I happen to meet some gorgeous hunk . . . well, that's just a bonus."

"A *big* bonus." Nancy grinned, glancing at her friend in the rearview mirror. Like George, she knew that unless Bess was seriously in love, meeting guys would always be the curvy, blue-eyed girl's number-one priority.

Whatever Bess's motives, though, Nancy was glad she was along. Both Bess and George were a big help whenever she was working on a case.

Smoothly Nancy brought the car to a stop at the end of the ramp, then turned toward the center of Emersonville. From her previous trips there, she knew they would have to drive through the town to get to the college.

Behind her, Bess was mildly ticked off over the ribbing she was getting. "You know, I'm not the only one with an ulterior motive for going on this trip," she grumbled.

"Are you referring to me?" George asked, playfully batting her lashes.

"You know it. I mean, what have *you* been talking about ever since we left River Heights? Nancy's case? No way! All you're concerned about is seeing a couple of big-deal basketball games."

"Well, can you blame me?" George said, suddenly growing defensive. "Emerson's the hottest team in the nation right now. If they win their last three games they'll grab their division title and go to the NCAA playoffs!"

Nancy smiled. Normally, George had a great sense of humor, but when it came to sports Bess's slender, dark-haired cousin was deadly serious.

"Besides," George added, grinning wickedly at Bess, "that's different. Basketball is what this case is all about."

"Maybe," Nancy stressed. "Coach Burnett wasn't too specific about what he wants me to investigate, remember?"

The night before Nancy had received a frantic call from Pat Burnett, the head coach of Emerson's top-ranked basketball team. Because he had been in a hurry, he hadn't been able to explain much. All he had said was that a highly unusual and extremely serious threat was facing his team. He needed her help badly, he had said.

Unable to resist his plea—or the promise of a new mystery to solve—Nancy had promised to round up her friends and drive down the very next day. It didn't matter to her that the details of the case were unclear. She'd learn them once she got to the college, she knew.

The three friends rode in silence for a few minutes. Outside the car, houses with snow-dusted lawns gradually gave way to Emersonville's business district, which was bustling in spite of the below-freezing temperature.

As she drove, Nancy's thoughts turned to her

own ulterior motive for taking this case—Ned Nickerson. Her boyfriend was an Emerson student and co-captain of the basketball team. It was going to be great to spend time with him, especially after the separations they had recently endured due to his schoolwork and her sleuthing.

A troubling question hung in her mind, however: Was Ned as excited about seeing her as she was about seeing him? Ordinarily, she would have been positive that he would be, but at the moment she wasn't so sure. Lately there had been some unsettling signs—letters that were less personal than before, phone calls that were shorter than their familiar talkathons. They were starting to drift apart, she felt, and that had her worried.

Beside her, George was stifling a laugh. "What's so funny?" Nancy asked.

"Oh, nothing much. You just drove by the main entrance to the college, that's all."

"What!" Nancy stomped on the brake pedal and swung the Mustang onto the shoulder. Glancing out the rear window, she saw that George was right: The entrance was at least a hundred yards behind them. She felt her cheeks grow warm. "Sorry. I guess I wasn't paying attention."

"Don't worry about it," Bess said. "Even detectives make mistakes."

"Especially when they've got their minds on other things," George added. "Like certain Emerson boys."

"You mean the ones whose names are spelled *N . . . e . . . d?*"

Now Nancy was really embarrassed. There was no point in denying that she had been thinking about Ned, though, she knew. Bess and George would see through her in a second.

For a moment she wondered whether to confess her fears to her friends, but quickly she decided against it. They were sure to tell her that she was worrying about nothing. And who could tell? Maybe she was. Anyway, there was only one way to find out. After checking the road in both directions, she gunned the car into a U-turn.

"Okay, I confess. Now quit the kidding, you guys, and help me find the sports center."

As it turned out, she didn't need any assistance. She remembered the way easily. The enormous building was on the far side of the campus beyond a cluster of science labs and next to the football field. Nancy spotted a parking space near the front entrance and turned into it.

"All right!" George said, zipping up her down-filled ski parka as she leapt out of the car. "This is what I like to see!"

"Yeah, a whole building devoted to self-torture," Bess finished. She pulled on a pair of pink wool mittens. "I don't understand it, George —don't you ever get tired of working out?"

"Nope!"

"Come on, let's get inside. It's freezing out

here," Nancy urged, locking her door. She was wearing jeans, boots, and a fleece-lined leather flight jacket, but even so the icy winter wind was making her shiver.

Inside, a security guard instructed them to sign the guest register, and a moment later they made their way into the main gymnasium. The basketball team was finishing their practice with a scrimmage. Sneakers squeaked on the polished wood floor as the players ran up and down the court.

It took Nancy a moment to spot her boyfriend. At six-feet-two, Ned stood out in most crowds, but among his supertall teammates he looked almost short. She hoped he would notice her on the sidelines, but it wasn't until a foul brought the action to a halt that he did.

"Hey, Nan," he called, sending her a half-hearted wave as he jogged over. "You made it. How was the drive down?"

A small lump formed in Nancy's throat. Some hello, she thought. Where were his usual "Hey there, gorgeous" and "It's great to see you"?

"The drive was fine," she managed to say. She waited for him to kiss her or give her a sweaty hug, but he didn't do either. Instead, he merely nodded at Bess and George.

"Glad you guys could make it. Come on, I'll introduce you to the coach."

Pat Burnett was a tall, silver-haired man in his late fifties. Nancy had seen him on the sidelines at games she had attended but had never met him before. His gray eyes shone with gratitude as he shook her hand. Standing with him was a stocky, pleasant-looking gentleman who appeared slightly older.

"This is Ed Riggs, our team physician," Ned said, introducing them. "Well, I guess I'd better get back on court."

"No, that's all for this afternoon," the coach pronounced. "Got to keep you fresh for tonight's game." Lifting his whistle, he blew a short blast. "Showers, everyone! And remember, I want you back here and in uniform no later than seven-thirty P.M."

The team drifted noisily toward the locker room. A few players walked past the sideline to get a closer look at the girls, and one—a tall, lanky, dark-haired boy—even stopped.

"What gives, Nickerson?" He grinned. "Hogging the girls for yourself?"

"Mike, this is Nancy Drew," Ned said. "Nancy, my co-captain, Mike O'Shea."

Nancy smiled politely as she shook hands. She had heard all about him from Ned: He was a senior, and the team's star forward. He and Ned were also fraternity brothers and good friends.

Mike beamed. "Ned's told me a lot about you. In fact, sometimes I think he doesn't know how to talk about anything else. How come you don't visit us more often?"

"Just busy, I guess," Nancy said, blushing. It felt good to know that Ned talked about her when she wasn't around. Maybe she *was* worrying over nothing.

Mike's question bothered her, though. Had Ned complained to him that she didn't visit enough?

A minute later the players were gone. The coach turned to Nancy and her friends. "Let's go to my office. We can talk more comfortably there. Ed, will you join us?" he asked the doctor.

"Certainly."

The coach's office was along the main corridor leading from the gym. Crammed with trophies, citations, and photographs, it was an impressive testimonial to a long and successful career. Dr. Riggs brought in extra chairs, and as he did Nancy felt a tingle of excitement run through her. Finally she was going to learn what this mystery was about!

"I'll get right to the point," the coach said, once they were all seated. "Someone is trying to ruin my team's chances of winning the division championship, and they're doing it with practical jokes."

Dr. Riggs nodded in agreement. "These aren't your average practical jokes, you understand. They are dangerous pranks that are intended to rattle the players' nerves. We know they're deliberate because they usually happen during games."

"Last Tuesday, for instance," the coach went on. "At halftime during our game against State, someone threw a smoke bomb into the locker room. My boys coughed themselves silly, and the second half was a disaster. Our rebound and foul-shot percentages were terrible. We won the game in the end, but not by much."

"The incident the week before was bad, too," Dr. Riggs said. "The boys arrived here for the game, only to find that the locker room had been trashed. Lockers were pulled over, and equipment was strewn everywhere. Someone had even slashed open a couple of balls."

"How awful!" George said.

The coach addressed Nancy. "Ned tells me that you're a whiz at getting to the bottom of things. Can you get to the bottom of this? I'd hate to lose the division title just because some fool upset my team."

Dr. Riggs agreed. "I'm retiring at the end of this season, Miss Drew, and I'd like nothing better than to leave on a winning note."

There was a short silence. Secretly, Nancy was disappointed. Finding a practical joker didn't seem like much of a challenge. She was used to tougher puzzles.

"Coach Burnett, tell me—why are you asking *me* to look into this? Can't the campus police handle it?" she asked.

"Evidently not," he said in disgust. "They did investigate for a while but got nowhere. Now they tell me they can't be bothered anymore . . . they've got more important matters to deal with."

"Oh?"

"Yes, it seems someone is picking out students at random and beating them up. Well, assaults are serious, but our problem is important, too. If we lose even one of our last three games, we'll lose the championship! That's why I took Ned's advice and called you, Nancy. These pranks have got to stop!"

Nancy knew that the pranks would probably stop on their own. Sooner or later most practical jokers lost interest in their activities. Still, telling that to the coach wasn't going to put his mind at rest. He wanted action *now*.

"Coach Burnett, have you told anyone else why I'm here?" she inquired.

"No, I thought it best not to mention it. That way you can pretend you're here to see the games, if it will help your investigation."

"It will." Because of Ned there was no hope of working undercover, but even so she wanted to remain as anonymous as possible.

Nancy was about to promise the coach that she would do her best when a commotion in the hall stopped her. Through the door they heard shouts and the sound of people running.

Crossing the room, Coach Burnett opened the door. Outside, Nancy could see members of the team dashing toward the gym. They were clad only in shorts, and from their expressions they were obviously upset.

"Jefferson!" the coach barked. "What's going on?"

A tall black player stopped by the door. His voice was tense. "I'm not sure, Coach, but the word is that somebody from the team just hung himself!"

Chapter

Two

INSTANTLY THE COACH bolted out the door and hurried after his team. Nancy and her friends were right behind him. It took only seconds to reach the gym, and as they entered it Nancy's stomach twisted in horror.

Hanging by a noose from one of the backboards was a human figure!

"Oh, no!" she heard George whisper behind her. Bess came up a moment later and stood next to them. "I don't believe it!" she gasped.

Nancy didn't either. She pushed her way through the players and stepped forward for a closer look. What she saw confirmed her suspicion: The figure wasn't human after all. It was an effigy—a dummy dressed in an Emerson basketball uniform.

Looking closer, she saw a sign pinned to its chest. It read: Death to the Wildcats!

"That's sick."

Ned was standing next to her, she realized. A look of disgust darkened his handsome, square-cut face.

"You said it!" Mike O'Shea spat, joining them. "Who'd do something like this?"

That was exactly the question on Nancy's mind. If this was supposed to be a joke, then it wasn't very funny. Turning away, she walked over to Coach Burnett, who was standing to one side with Dr. Riggs. Both men were shaking their heads.

"The sooner I get to work on this the better," Nancy said quietly. "Do you think you can get this gym cleared out?"

"Sure thing," the coach replied. "Okay, guys! You've seen what there is to see. Let's move out!"

The team started back to the locker room slowly. Nancy saw many unhappy looks and overheard the words "jinx" and "bad luck" as the players muttered to one another in low tones.

Coach Burnett was following his team out when Nancy stopped him. "That uniform the effigy is wearing . . . how could the joker have gotten hold of it?" she asked.

"Probably bought it." The coach shrugged. "That's not our official uniform—just a copy that anyone can purchase at the student bookstore."

"You're sure? It couldn't have been stolen from someone on the team?"

"No, we've never used that number."

"Okay, thanks, Coach Burnett. I'll let you know the second I've got any solid leads."

When the gym was finally empty, Nancy held a conference with Bess and George.

"First we've got to establish how the joker got in. George, you check every door to the building. I want to know whether they're locked."

"But there must be dozens!" George objected. "How will I find them all?"

"Walk around the outside of the building. That'll be fastest," Nancy suggested. "Bess, you check out the front entrance. Find out who signed the guest register today and whether someone without an Emerson ID could have slipped in."

"You got it, Nan."

While her friends were busy with their assignments, Nancy borrowed a ladder and a knife from a janitor, cut down the effigy, and examined it. It was crudely sewn from a set of one-piece long underwear. Its head was part of a plain white pillowcase. Inside, it was stuffed with Styrofoam packing chips. No clues there, Nancy decided. Anyone could have assembled the materials.

She was studying the note pinned to the effigy's chest when her friends returned.

"The exits can only be opened from the inside," George reported. "Whoever did this was either let in or came in through the front entrance."

"Good work. Bess?"

"The guard claims that security is extra tight because of those assaults the coach mentioned. Only students with Emerson ID cards can get in."

"What about the guest register? Any names down for today?"

"Yes, three . . . Nancy Drew, George Fayne, and Bess Marvin. That's it."

"Terrific." Nancy groaned. "That blows my first theory. I figured the joker might be someone connected with a rival team, but since it's impossible to sneak in here that idea is out."

"The joker could still have been let in through a side exit by someone else," George reasoned.

Nancy shook her head. "I don't think so. Practical jokers don't usually work in pairs. My guess is that the culprit came in through the front entrance with the dummy hidden in a gym bag."

"But, Nancy!" Bess was horrified. "If that's true it means—"

"Yes. The practical joker is someone from Emerson College!"

A short while later Ned appeared. In his jeans and crisp shirt, his hair still damp from the shower, Nancy thought he looked fantastic. She wanted to throw her arms around him, but his grim expression made it clear that he was in no mood for fun.

"Think you can track down this clown?" he

asked as Nancy drove to the dormitory in which Ned had arranged for the girls to stay.

"It shouldn't be too hard."

"Yes, with Nancy on the case the creep'll be caught in no time," Bess said from the backseat.

"I hope so. These incidents are getting on everyone's nerves."

"Yours, too?" Nancy teased lightly.

"No, but I can understand why some of the guys are upset. We're under a lot of pressure, and the practical jokes just add to it."

"I can imagine," George remarked. "It must be like waiting for bombs to explode, except that you never know when or where they'll go off."

"Exactly."

Two more turns brought them to the dormitory, a modern brick-and-glass building by a parking lot. Ned helped them unload their gear, then began to carry Nancy's duffel bag and Bess's suitcase toward the side entrance.

"Ned, you can't go in there with us!" Nancy said.

"Sure I can. Didn't I tell you?" He grinned. "It's a coed dorm!"

George chuckled. "Hear that, Bess? You should love it here."

"Will you please knock it off? How many times do I have to tell you? I'm not here to hunt guys," Bess declared. "Anyway, who cares? It's strictly buddy-buddy in coed dorms, right, Ned?"

"So I hear," he confirmed.

Their room was on the third floor. It was part of a suite that had its own bathroom and kitchenette. Nancy loved it.

"Who usually lives here?" she asked.

"It's a spare suite," Ned informed her. "The school keeps it for special visitors." He handed them each a key to the room and another to the dorm's side entrance.

Nancy tossed her duffel bag at the foot of one of the beds, then walked with Ned to the door. "Thanks," she said softly. "Uh, Ned . . . any chance we can get together while I'm here?"

"I was going to ask you the same thing. Won't you be pretty busy tackling this case?"

"Not *that* busy, I hope."

"Good." He smiled. "Omega Chi Epsilon is having a party tonight after the game. Care to go with me?"

Happiness flooded through her. "You bet!" She grinned. "Can Bess and George go, too?"

"Of course. Just wait for me outside the gym after the game, okay?"

"*Okay!*"

He kissed her then. It was nothing heavy—just a "see you later" sort of kiss—but it was enough for Nancy. Her heart soared.

"Will you look at the size of that crowd!" Bess whistled in amazement.

The three girls were walking toward the sports complex for that evening's game against St.

George's College. A noisy line several hundred people long stretched from the main entrance to the middle of the parking lot. Homemade banners and purple-and-orange Emerson pennants were everywhere.

"Gee, I hope we'll be able to get in!" George said.

"We will, don't worry. The gym holds at least four thousand," Nancy told her.

"Good," Bess put in, "but where are the other team's supporters going to sit?"

"Outside, if the Emerson fans have anything to say about it."

As they joined the line, however, Nancy noticed that not everyone was there to cheer on the rival teams. Up near the doors, which were not yet open, a group of sign-carrying students was staging a protest. She could hear jeering voices from the crowd, urging them to get lost.

"I wonder what's going on?" she said curiously.

"Why don't you and George check it out? I'll hold our places," Bess offered.

"Thanks. Let's go."

As she and George drew close, Nancy saw that the signs the protesters carried read "Say 'No' to Burnett's Budget!" and "Scholarship Before Sports!" The protesters seemed discouraged by the crowd's hostility, but their leader—a brown-haired, confident-looking boy—was determined to continue the demonstration.

"C'mon . . . we can't give up yet!" he roared.

"Hey . . . how about you two girls? Will you sign our petition?" He thrust a clipboard at Nancy and George.

Nancy glanced at the letter it held. There were only half a dozen signatures on it. "Uh . . . I don't know. What does it say?"

"It demands that the trustees assign less money to the Physical Education department in next year's budget."

George bristled. "Why should they do that? Physical education is important!"

"Sure, but not more important than academics. Yet each year the P.E. department gets more money than any other. It's not fair."

"Yes it is," George countered. "Sports programs are expensive."

The boy's face darkened. "Oh, I get it—you're a jock. You care more about the locker room than about the classroom."

"And you'd rather grind than unwind!" George shot back. "Tell me something—what makes you think you know what's best for this school?"

"Well, for one thing I'm president of the student council. Tom Stafford's the name, in case you didn't know."

"I didn't. But I still say sports are important."

"Typical," Tom said, turning away in disgust. "You jocks are all alike—all brawn, no brains."

Now Nancy was angry, too. She believed strongly in free speech, but the student leader's last remark was too much.

19

"That's not fair. I know plenty of athletes who are also excellent students," she said.

Tom pivoted. "Sure. Name one!"

"My boyfriend, Ned Nickerson."

The change that came over Tom at the mention of Ned's name was striking. Suddenly his eyes narrowed. His voice grew cold. "You go out with the Big Nick, huh? Well, congratulations. I hope you're enjoying your share of the school's money."

"My *what?*" Nancy asked, astonished.

"You know what I'm talking about," Tom hinted darkly. "Tell me, do you and Ned toast the trustees when you're out on the town?"

"Just what are you implying?" she demanded. "What do our dates have to do with trustees or school money or *anything?*"

George tugged on her arm. "Come on, Nancy, this guy's a jerk. Let's go."

"Not until he explains himself! He's insulting Ned! And I'm not going to let him get away with it!"

"Nancy, come *on!* The line's beginning to move."

Reluctantly, Nancy abandoned her argument with Tom Stafford and rejoined the line. In no time they were inside, climbing the bleachers to their seats. She explained what had happened to Bess, who agreed that Tom was out of his mind.

"How someone like that could be elected president of the student council is beyond me," she remarked.

"Me, too."

Nancy seethed quietly. Once the game began, however, she gradually forgot the encounter. The action was fast and exciting, and it was impossible not to be swept up by it.

St. George's had a good team, but they were no match for Emerson's razzle-dazzle offense and their tough, relentless defense. Several times Ned took possession on the rebound and led his team in fast break drives down the court. The score climbed, and by the end of the first half Emerson was ahead by an eighteen-point margin.

"Looks like the game's in the bag," Nancy said to George during halftime.

"Sure looks that way." George grinned back.

But a few minutes later Nancy realized she had spoken too soon. Shortly after the jump ball that began the second half, the action came to a halt as a blood-curdling scream rang out!

Chapter

Three

AN EERIE SILENCE descended in the gym. It
didn't last, however. A second later a murmur
rose from the bleachers. On the court, a referee
blew his whistle for a time-out. Nancy noticed
security guards hurrying toward the Emerson
bench, and without a moment's hesitation she
joined them.

The scream had come from the pretty, freckle-
faced student who masqueraded as the team mascot, the Emerson Wildcat, Nancy discovered. The
girl was standing behind the bench in tears. She
wore the Wildcat costume, minus the head, but it
hung from her limbs in tatters.

It had been slashed to ribbons!

"I don't understand. . . . I only had it off for a few minutes!" the girl sobbed. "I was taking a break, and . . . and when I put it back on . . . " Her sobs grew louder.

"Don't worry, it isn't your fault," the head cheerleader consoled her. "It could have happened to anyone."

Nancy pushed through the crowd around the unhappy girl. "Excuse me . . . where did you put the costume while you were on your break?"

"In the cheerleaders' locker room, as always," the girl said, wiping her eyes with her fingers.

"Was the room locked?"

"No, it never is, as far as I know."

"Did you notice anyone hanging around in the corridor outside it?"

"No! The hall was empty and so was the locker room."

"Too bad," Nancy muttered. Obviously, the practical joker had struck again. She had hoped to gain some clues to his or her identity, but it appeared that none had been left.

Disappointed, she turned away. As she did, she saw that the team members were staring at the damage to their mascot. Their expressions ranged from shock to fear. Probably they were wondering if the next practical joke would involve one of *them* being slashed, she guessed.

Someone else was looking at the damage, too,

she discovered a moment later—Tom Stafford. He was hovering inconspicuously at the edge of the crowd, but thanks to her earlier encounter with him she picked him out right away. Could he have slashed the costume? There was no way to be sure, of course, but the satisfied expression on his face made her very suspicious.

Nancy decided to question him. By the time she reached the spot where he had been standing, however, he was gone.

When the game began again it quickly became clear that Emerson had lost its edge. St. George's scored three times in less than one minute, and a series of fouls by Emerson players only made the situation worse. With ten minutes left, Emerson's lead had dropped to a slim four points.

Nancy cheered herself hoarse. If Emerson didn't pull together soon, she knew, they'd lose the game—and with it their chances of making the NCAA playoffs.

The score seesawed, but finally, with just five minutes left to play, Emerson began to rally. Coach Burnett called for a full court press—an aggressive defense pattern. It was a risky move, but it worked. Frustrated, St. George's lost its momentum. The rhythm of the game shifted. Once again Emerson regained the upper hand. When the final buzzer sounded, the score was Emerson 79, St. George's 73.

Afterward, Nancy and her friends went with Ned to his fraternity, Omega Chi Epsilon, for the victory celebration.

"All right, let's *party!*" George said as they entered the darkened, jam-packed common room.

"You said it. That game was tense. I need to relax," Bess agreed.

The two snaked their way through the noisy crowd to the refreshment table. Nancy stayed where she was, staring blankly at the partyers. She felt Ned's hand on her shoulder.

"Everything okay? You aren't in much of a party mood," he observed.

Nancy smiled apologetically. "Sorry, I guess my mind's still on the game."

"Why? We won, didn't we?"

"Sure, but you almost lost because of that so-called practical joke. I should have known something like that was going to happen."

"Nancy, you couldn't have prevented it."

"Maybe not, but if I had been prepared I might have picked up some clues! As it stands, I've got exactly one suspect and zero evidence."

Ned lowered his eyebrows. "Lighten up on yourself, will you? You've only been on the case for a few hours! You'll crack it."

"I know. I just hope I crack it before another disaster occurs."

"Well, there won't be any disasters at this party, that much I know. In fact, I have a feeling that something nice is about to happen to you."

"Oh, yes?" Nancy felt a smile tug at the corners of her mouth. "Like what?"

"Come here and I'll show you."

She expected him to kiss her, but that wasn't what he had in mind. Instead he took her hand and led her to a quiet corner. They sat together on an overstuffed sofa.

"Here, this is for you." Reaching into the pocket of his jacket, Ned pulled out a small package. It was wrapped in white paper and tied with a pink ribbon.

"Ned, you shouldn't have!"

"It's something to help you remember this visit. Go on. Open it!"

Nancy's fingers shook as she unwrapped the gift. It was a delicate silver bracelet, the loveliest she had ever seen. She slid it on.

"It's beautiful! But, Ned, it must have cost a fortune!"

Her boyfriend's face darkened for a split second. Was he angry? Troubled? Before she could decide, the look faded.

"The price doesn't matter. I want you to have it. I've missed you, Nancy."

A lump formed in her throat. "I've missed you, too. And how!"

She threw her arms around him and kissed him—sweetly at first, but then with growing urgency. It felt terrific to be with him again! Silently she vowed not to wait so long between visits the next time.

Suddenly a chorus of voices interrupted them.

"Hey, Nickers, save it for later!"

"Yeah, it's party time!"

"Ned . . . can you hear us, Ned? Uh-oh, looks like we've lost him. Send for an ambulance!"

They fell apart. Around them stood a group of Ned's teammates, all grinning mischievously. Nancy stood and tried—unsuccessfully—not to blush as Ned introduced them.

"Nancy, this is Andy Hall . . ."

She shook the hand of a black youth with a narrow, baby-smooth face. He was the off-guard, she knew, Ned's opposite number on the Wildcats' starting lineup.

". . . and Craig Watson . . ."

Tall, blond, and amazingly cute, Craig was the power forward, or "enforcer," who did the work that made the others look good.

". . . and our center, Howie Little."

Nancy's eyes traveled up . . . and up . . . and up . . . to the face of the tallest boy she had ever met. Howie Little was a towering seven-feet-one. He had deep black skin and sparkling eyes, which were full of humor.

"Hello down there," he said, laughing. His voice was a deep bass, like the lowest notes on a church organ. "It's kind of hard to tell from this distance, Ned, but it looks to me like you've got yourself one pretty girlfriend there."

Everyone laughed, Nancy hardest of all. She liked Howie's sense of humor.

"Where's Mike?" Ned asked, looking around for his friend.

Craig pointed. "Over there. He's still upset about what happened during the game, I guess."

All eyes turned to a couple across the room. Nancy saw Mike O'Shea talking with a short, snub-nosed brunette. His girlfriend, probably. She looked as if she was trying to calm him down. It wasn't working, however. As they watched, Mike pulled away from her and stalked out of the room.

"Mike takes those practical jokes kind of hard," Ned explained to Nancy in a low voice. "Tonight, for instance, after the mascot's costume was slashed he could barely dribble the ball."

"Maybe he's high-strung," Nancy said.

"Strung *out* is more like it," Andy drawled sourly.

"What do you mean?"

Ned shot Andy a warning look. "All he means is that Mike's been feeling run-down, lately. We've all been feeling run-down! It's been a long, tough season."

Murmurs of agreement followed his remark, but Nancy caught an undercurrent of tension in the air. Were they upset over Mike's poor performance in that night's game, or was there more to it than that? And why was Ned covering up for him? That was very unusual!

Nancy's thoughts were interrupted by a new

voice—one that was high, thin, and tinged with an unpleasant edge of sarcasm.

"Aren't you going to introduce *me*, too?"

"Ray, what are you doing here?" Ned asked.

The newcomer was tall and skinny. He had pale blue eyes, a prominent hooked nose, and red hair that needed to be trimmed. He stared at Nancy.

"I thought you wanted nothing more to do with the Wildcats," Ned added.

"I don't. You can all rot, for all I care. I like a good party, though. So . . . are you going to introduce me, or not?"

"Nancy, this is Ray Ungar. Ray, my girlfriend, Nancy Drew."

Ray's eyes bored into hers. Nancy was used to being checked out, but his reckless expression made her very uneasy.

"So, you're the famous snoop Ned's always bragging about."

"I've solved a few crimes," Nancy said noncommittally.

"A few? Ned makes you sound like a regular Sherlock Holmes. Well, take a tip from me, Ms. Sherlock . . . watch where you poke your nose here at Emerson. It might get cut off."

"Can it, Ray!" Ned said angrily, taking a step toward him. "I know you're carrying a grudge, but take it out on someone else!"

Ray held up his palms. "Hey! I was just giving the lady some advice!"

"Well, save it. In fact, why don't you move along and enjoy the party?"

"Sure, I know when I'm not wanted." Throwing a hostile glance at Andy, Craig, and Howie, he sauntered away.

Nancy was relieved. "Whew! Talk about intense! What's his problem, anyway? And what's all this about a grudge?"

"Ray used to be on the team," Ned explained. "He wasn't a starter, but he wasn't bad as a forward, either."

"*Used* to be?"

"Coach cut him this season because he's got a low grade-point average. Now he's bitter. He swears Coach cut him for personal reasons."

"Sounds like he really hates the team."

"That's the understatement of the semester!" Ned agreed grimly. "He won't even come to our games to cheer us on!"

The group gradually drifted apart. As it did, Nancy remembered what she had said to Ned earlier about having only one suspect. Well, scratch that, she thought. Now I have two!

The party wore on, growing louder and wilder by the minute. Nancy met many more of Ned's friends, including Mike's girlfriend, Jan Teller. Finally, around midnight, she went to the refreshment table to pour herself a soda. Bess was there, too, taking a break.

"Having fun?" Nancy asked.

"Believe it!" Bess smiled. "They really know how to party here."

"Did I see you dancing with Craig Watson a little while ago?"

Bess's eyes grew misty. "Yes. He's a great guy. Soooo cute! And such a sharp dresser, too . . . did you notice?"

Nancy hadn't. Glancing across the room, she saw Craig talking to Ned. In his loose-fitting gray wool shirt, pleated flannel trousers, and Gucci loafers, he indeed looked sharp. He could have posed for a layout in a fashion magazine.

"Matter of fact, a lot of these basketball guys have style," Bess went on.

"Really? Who else?"

"Mike and Andy, see?"

The two players were talking together at the other end of the table. Both were dressed very well, Nancy realized. Andy wore an Italian-cut silk suit, and a gold watch flashed on Mike's wrist.

She frowned. "That's odd . . . didn't I read in the game program that Craig, Andy, and Mike are scholarship students?"

"Did you? I don't know."

"Hmmm . . . I'll check it out when we get back to our room."

A second later, though, Nancy forgot all about that idea. The disk jockey put on a favorite song of

31

Ned's, and suddenly she wanted to dance. Setting down her drink, she crossed the room and pulled her boyfriend onto the dance floor.

They danced for what seemed like hours. Finally, flushed and happy, Nancy realized that she was worn out. She also needed the bathroom. Excusing herself, she went down the hall, only to find a short line in front of it.

Deciding that she couldn't wait, she slipped up the stairs to the second floor. Doors lined both sides of the hall, but which one was the bathroom? She didn't know.

Nancy chose a door at random. She knocked, and—receiving no answer—pushed it open.

"Oops!"

It was a fraternity brother's room, empty at the moment, luckily. She was about to shut the door and go when, in the light from the hall, she noticed a framed picture above the desk. It was of Mike and Ned! This wasn't Ned's room, she knew. She had seen that before, so it must be Mike's.

Curious, she moved toward the photo for a closer look. As she did, she accidentally kicked a cardboard carton. She looked down—and gasped. It was full of Styrofoam packing chips!

Rooting among them, Nancy also found scraps of cloth, thread, and the mangled half of a pillowcase—the same materials used to construct the effigy! She was stunned. There could only

be one conclusion, she knew: Mike O'Shea
—Emerson's best player—was the practical joker!

Suddenly, the door behind her creaked. Nancy
whirled and stifled a scream. A tall, threatening
figure was silhouetted in the doorway!

Chapter
Four

W HAT ARE YOU doing in here?" Ned demanded. He flicked the light switch next to the door.

Nancy blinked. "Oh, it's you! Thank goodness . . . you startled me."

"Nancy? I said, what are you doing poking around in Mike's room?"

There was a coolness in his tone that puzzled her. Why was he being so hostile? It wasn't as if she'd been doing anything wrong!

"I came upstairs for the bathroom but walked in here by mistake," she explained. "But I'm glad I did. Look what I found!"

She nudged the carton toward him with her

toe. Ned glanced at its contents and shrugged.
"So?"

"Don't you see? It's the same stuff that was used to make the dummy in the gym!" Quickly she filled him in on her examination of the effigy. "It means that Mike is behind all the practical jokes!"

"Not necessarily."

Nancy stared at him, unable to believe what she was hearing. "Come on, Ned, be serious . . . what else could it mean?"

"Well, maybe it's just a coincidence. Or maybe somebody dropped that box in here in order to frame him."

Nancy thought about that. At first she was embarrassed—she had jumped to a conclusion! But then she realized that she had been right after all.

"No, it couldn't be a frame-up," she reasoned. "A frame-up would be more obvious. Think about it . . . why dump the evidence in a place where only *Mike* is likely to find it?"

"Okay, I'll admit it sounds farfetched," Ned said. "But so what? It's not as farfetched as *your* theory!"

"What do you mean?"

"I mean that I know Mike. He'd never do anything to hurt the team."

"Are you sure about that?"

"Of course I am! The Wildcats mean everything to him. He'd no more play practical jokes on us than . . . well, than he would shoot the ball into the other team's basket!"

A short silence followed. Ned had a point, Nancy knew. There was no good reason for Emerson's co-captain to undermine the team's morale, none that she could think of, anyway. On the contrary, he had every reason to work for the team's success! Was her theory a washout after all?

No, she decided, the evidence was right in front of them. Maybe she didn't know the motive yet, but she couldn't ignore the facts. Somehow she had to convince Ned that she might be right.

"Ned, maybe someone's *paying* Mike to play the practical jokes," she suggested.

Ned shook his head. "Give me a break. Even if Mike could be bribed, which I doubt, who would do something like that?"

"A rival team?"

"No way! Those pranks have been played before and during *all* our games."

"Okay, then maybe Mike's got his own reason . . . a secret one. Maybe it's even a subconscious desire to lose, or something."

"You're way off base," Ned declared. "Mike and I are friends. If he were loony-tunes, believe me, I'd know!"

Nancy was getting ticked off. "Ned, why are you being so stubborn? You've got solid evidence of Mike's guilt right at your feet!"

Ned crossed his arms. "You know as well as I do that evidence can be misleading. To pin the blame on someone you need more than a box of packing chips—you need a motive, too!"

"Okay, okay!"

Nancy began to pace back and forth. Usually she was calm and collected when working on a case, but now she was beginning to feel frustration. She didn't like it.

"All right, I guess we'll have to investigate some more," she said finally. "Here's where we'll start—"

"We?" Ned interrupted.

"Of course." She stopped pacing and glanced at him. "Ned, you're going to help me, aren't you?" she asked.

"Help you what? Dig up dirt on my friend? No, I'm not."

Nancy was stunned. "You've got to be kidding me! Come on, Ned, you're in a perfect position to help. You're inside the team! Anyway, you've never refused to help before."

"You've never suspected one of my friends before, either."

Her temples began to throb. Rubbing them, she muttered, "I can't believe what I'm hearing. Are you telling me that you don't want to put a stop to the practical joker?"

"Of course I do!" he growled angrily.

"Then help me!"

"Show me a suspect with a good motive and I will!"

"This box—"

"Forget the box! That's not a motive. That's just a clue!"

He was working himself into a rage. His dark eyes were blazing. His jaw was tight. Nancy had never seen him look at her that way before—not once!

"What's with you, anyway?" he said furiously. "Sometimes I think you care more about solving mysteries than you do about people."

"That's not fair!" she cried. "It's *people* that I'm trying to help . . . people like Coach Burnett and the members of your team."

"Yeah, well, it won't do any good to come down on a guy with no motive."

"Then what should I do? Trust him?"

"Sure."

"Forget it. He'll just pull more practical jokes." Ned was disgusted. "C'mon. You're not even sure he's responsible."

"And you're not sure that he isn't!"

It was a stalemate. She couldn't see it Ned's way, and Ned wouldn't see it hers. What was she going to do?

First of all she would remain calm, she decided. Next she would try hard to see it from Ned's point of view. For a full minute she studied the toes of her boots, trying to understand what Ned saw that she did not. She failed. Every way she looked at it, her conclusion was still the same—the evidence pointed to Mike!

"I don't know. I can't believe we're arguing like this," she said finally.

Ned's voice was hollow. "Me either. How come you're so determined to nail Mike?"

"I'm not trying to nail him. All I'm saying is that we should investigate some more!"

"No." Ned shook his head sadly. "Mike's my buddy, and I'm going to stick by him. This time you're on your own."

"Ned, *please!* I need you on this case!"

"Like I said, you've got me . . . but not to throw dirt on my friend," he insisted.

Nancy's anger returned full force. She kicked the cardboard carton. "Ned, you're letting me down! Why can't you open your eyes? Why can't you use your head!"

"Logic isn't the only way to get at the truth," Ned said softly. "Sometimes you have to listen to your heart."

It was a long time before Nancy was able to think of a reply. When she did, it was too late. Ned was gone.

A short while later, Nancy, Bess, and George walked back to their dorm. It was bitterly cold and very quiet. Their feet crunched on the hard-packed snow. Their breath made frosty white clouds in the air.

Nancy tried to conceal her feelings, but her

friends sensed that something was wrong. Soon she had told them the entire story, from her earlier fears about her and Ned to their argument in Mike's room.

For once the cousins had little to say.

"I sure hope you can patch things up," Bess said in a small voice.

"Thanks. Me, too," Nancy replied. "I just don't understand why he's being so stubborn. The evidence was right under his nose!"

George sighed. "I guess he's doing what he feels is right."

"I guess."

All the windows in the dorm were dark. When they reached the side entrance, Bess whipped out her key and dashed inside. George held the door open for Nancy.

"Aren't you coming in?"

"No, I'm going to stay outside for a while and look at the stars. I've got some things to sort out, you know?"

"I think I do. See you upstairs."

Letting out a long breath, Nancy stuffed her hands in the pockets of her jacket. What a mess! The idea of tackling this case without Ned—worse, without his support—made her feel awful. What should she do?

Maybe she should give up and go home, she reflected. She hated to let Coach Burnett down, but at the same time nothing was worth the misery she was going through. And anyway, it was just a bunch of practical jokes, wasn't it? Nothing serious.

Just then Bess burst out the door. Startled, Nancy stared at her in alarm.

"Nan," Bess gasped, "we've got to go back to River Heights right away!"

Chapter
Five

WHAT! WHY?"

Bess's face was pale. "Never mind why! Just warm up your car. We've got to get out of here as soon as possible!"

Nancy ran her fingers through her reddish gold hair. Great, she thought. Now, on top of everything else, Bess was freaking out! What could have made her so upset?

"Bess, calm down, okay? Try to tell me what happened."

"Oh, Nancy, it's awful. The room . . . our clothes . . . what if we hadn't gone to the party? *What if we had been there!*"

The room? A feeling of dread shot through

Nancy. Brushing past her friend, she unlocked the entrance and raced up the stairs. She saw right away why Bess had freaked.

The room was a mess. The door had been jimmied, and their clothes were strewn everywhere. Desks and chairs were overturned. The bed coverings had been torn off. Nancy felt sick. Who could have done this? she wondered. A burglar? A vandal?

It was neither. Alerted by the smell of paint, she whirled around. There, spray painted on the room's large plate-glass window, was a bloodred warning: Go Home, Drew!

So! The practical joker was on to her!

Bess came in behind her. "See what I mean? Let's get out of here, Nancy."

"No way!" she declared. Her fists curled in anger. "You can split if you want to, but I'm going to stay as long as it takes."

"But our stuff . . . the room . . . ! As soon as we report this, the school is going to throw us out anyway, I just know it."

"I doubt that. The mess can be straightened up, and the paint will come off. They'll let us stay. By the way, where's George?"

"She went for a security guard," Bess said.

A minute later George returned with both the guard and the dorm advisor, a senior named Lynn. Lynn was horrified but assured Nancy that they could remain.

"Your boyfriend vouched for you girls when he

43

arranged for the room. I know this isn't your fault. It could have happened to anyone."

That wasn't exactly true, Nancy knew, but she decided not to mention it. Instead, she zeroed in on the cleanup.

"Some turpentine would help that window. Is there any in the building?"

"Yes, in the basement," Lynn confirmed. "I'll get it."

When she was gone, the guard conducted a brief investigation. The moment he had enough information for his report, he stuffed his pen back into his shirt pocket.

"No permanent damage to school property, fortunately," he remarked. "Sorry about your clothes, though."

"Me, too. Any chance of having that lock fixed tonight?" Nancy asked.

"Yes. I'll phone the central maintenance office and have them send their night man right over," he offered.

"Thanks. Oh, one more thing. Any idea how the . . . uh . . . vandal got into the building?"

The guard scratched his head. "Well, the front door is guarded around the clock, so I guess he came in the side entrance, same as you."

"But I have a key!"

"So do lots of people. There are one hundred kids living in this dorm, miss. It's fairly common for them to copy their keys for their friends. Anybody could get one easily."

"I see. Thank you."

Rats! she thought. No help there. Why were clues so hard to come by on this case? Either the practical joker was very lucky, or he had more on the ball than she thought!

The next morning, Nancy and her friends ate breakfast in the student union. Bess still wanted to return to River Heights, but after an hour of heavy persuasion Nancy was able to convince her to stay.

"You're sure we're not in any danger?" Bess asked for the third time.

"I'm positive. Look, you have to understand how practical jokers think . . . they don't get their kicks from injuring people. They make their victims suffer in other ways."

"Oh, thanks. Now I feel a *lot* better!"

"Take it easy, will you?" George snapped. "Why can't you stop worrying for once?"

"Fine. I will. The next time someone wants to wreck our room I'll let them in and give them a hand, okay?"

"Don't be melodramatic."

"Well, what do you want me to do?"

"Relax!" George picked up her tray. "Come explore the campus with us! We might as well enjoy ourselves while we can, right?"

"I suppose."

Bundled against the cold, the three girls began a self-guided tour. Emerson's ivy-covered buildings looked lovely in the snow, but Nancy's mind was on the case. What she needed now was a plan, she knew. The practical joker was on the alert. In order to catch him, she would have to outwit him—but how?

There was another problem on her mind, too—Ned. She still believed that Mike O'Shea was the number-one suspect, but she could see now that she had pushed too hard the night before. Not only had she attacked Ned's teammate, she had attacked Ned's judgment, too! Somehow she would have to convince him that she still respected him, she decided.

As they entered the student bookstore, Nancy stopped at the bank of pay phones just inside the door.

"Go ahead," she told her friends. "I'll join you after I call Ned."

She dug a quarter from her purse, then held it near the coin slot as she thought about what to say. As she did, however, her attention was caught by a handsome, dark-haired boy hurrying to a nearby phone. What a hunk! she thought. Who was he calling? Some lucky girl, no doubt.

But he wasn't calling a girl. At least, it didn't sound that way.

"Hello, this is Captain Hook."

Captain Hook? What was this all about? Nancy wondered.

The boy continued: "What's the line for tomorrow? Yeah? Well, let me have a ten-timer. No . . . the other guys."

Stranger and stranger! Nancy knew it wasn't polite to eavesdrop, but she couldn't help herself —especially not when the conversation was this interesting!

"What do you mean I can't have it?" His face was turned away from her, but his tone was clearly annoyed. "C'mon, man!" A pause. "Look, Frank will cover for me, okay?"

That was it. With a hasty "Thanks," he hung up and rushed off.

Nancy was more puzzled than ever. What did all that mumbo-jumbo mean? Well, she didn't have time to figure it out. She had something more important to do: save her relationship with Ned!

Dropping the coin into the slot, she dialed his number. Their conversation was short. Ned was on his way to an economics class. They set up a date for that evening, however. They could see a movie in town, he suggested. Afterward, they could go to his favorite pizza joint.

"That sounds fine. Listen, Ned . . ." Nancy hesitated, toying with some loose change and a scrap of paper she'd found on the ledge under the phone. There was so much she wanted to say. Where should she begin?

Ned cut her off. "Save it, Nancy. I've got to run."

"Sure, 'bye."

Nancy's heart sank as she hung up the receiver. He sounded so cool! Would he ever forgive her for the way she had acted?

Nancy absentmindedly scooped the change into her purse. The scrap of paper fell in with it, and Nancy noticed vaguely that a phone number was written on it. Captain Hook must have dropped it. She didn't stop to think about it, though. Instead, she rushed worriedly from the booth.

That evening, Ned picked her up at eight. It was their worst date ever, Nancy decided later. The movie was terrible, and at the raucous pizza parlor they sat across from one another awkwardly, hardly talking, the only unhappy-looking couple in the entire place.

Nancy felt miserable. Ned hated her guts, she was sure of it. When he looked up from his third sausage-and-mushroom slice, she waited nervously for him to speak.

"So, where are Bess and George tonight?" he asked.

"George went to the sports complex to work out," Nancy explained. "Bess is with her."

A smile tugged at the corners of Ned's mouth. "Bess went to the gym voluntarily?"

"Uh-huh." Nancy smiled, too. "She said she didn't want to be alone in the room after the break-in last night, soooo . . ."

"Amazing. Maybe some good will come out of this case after all."

"If you think Bess will discover the joys of working out tonight, forget it. She only went because she was desperate."

Suddenly, Nancy couldn't stand the tension in the air for another second. Leaning on her elbows, she stared deep into his eyes.

"Ned, can we talk? I mean, really *talk*? I acted like a jerk last night, and I'm sorry. Please say you'll forgive me!"

Ned leaned back in his chair, a satisfied look on his face. "Of course I forgive you," he said. "I'm glad you see how wrong you were, too. Mike's my buddy, and—"

"Wait a minute! Hold on! I didn't say I was *wrong*. Not about Mike. What I said was, I acted dumb."

Ned cooled visibly. "Then you still suspect him of being the practical joker?"

"Of course. The stuff in that carton—"

"Nancy, I can't believe this!" Ned exploded. "Doesn't it matter to you that I've known Mike for two years? Don't you care that he's my friend and that I trust him?"

"Sure I do! That's what I'm trying to say . . . I was stupid to question your judgment last night. I shouldn't have argued like that."

Ned cocked his head warily. "So you'll back off on investigating him?"

"No, but—"

"Then don't bother to apologize. Nothing has changed."

"Ned, please!"

He shook his head. "I'm sorry. Maybe you think I'm a dumb jock, but I believe in supporting my team. I play on their side until the game is over."

Nancy's heart ached. She didn't think of Ned as a "dumb jock." He was loyal and dependable and fierce when their backs were against a wall. She loved those qualities in him—and now they were tearing them apart!

Nancy felt even worse when Ned dropped her off at the dorm. He didn't kiss her. They didn't hug. Instead, she merely stood in the middle of the parking lot, watching the taillights of his car disappear around a corner.

Now what was she going to do? she wondered. She couldn't give up the case, not after last night. But she couldn't stand what was happening to her and Ned, either!

Suddenly, a sharp sound spun her around. As she watched, a man burst from a side entrance to a nearby dorm. He ran to a black Camaro, hopped in, and gunned the engine.

The next second, the Camaro was heading for her at top speed!

Chapter

Six

NANCY COULDN'T BELIEVE it. He was going to run her down!

Reacting instinctively, she dove. It was just like diving into a pool, except that she rolled as she hit. Headlights swept the pavement. Tires swished past her head. The Camaro missed her by inches!

Furious, Nancy leapt to her feet. She wanted the Camaro's license number! But its rear lights were out, she noticed. As it fishtailed on an icy patch and turned the corner, all she could see was a menacing black wedge disappearing into the night. Then it was gone.

Nancy's breath came fast and hard. Her heart

pounded. No way was she going to back off now! she resolved. Not after an attempt on her life! How long had the guy been waiting in the warmth of the dorm for her to appear? An hour? Two?

Off in the distance, a siren began to wail. As it came closer, she gradually realized what had actually happened. The Camaro hadn't been after her. Its driver had been making a getaway. And his first victim—or maybe a witness—must have telephoned the police.

Sure enough, a minute later a squad car pulled into the lot, its roof lights twirling. Two campus policemen jumped out and raced into the dorm— the same dorm from which she had seen the Camaro driver run.

Nancy followed. It didn't take long to find the trouble. In the stairwell lay a male student, about eighteen years old, she judged. He was still breathing, but not very well. He had been worked over by a pro.

More police arrived. As they did, she recalled the apparently random assaults that Coach Burnett had mentioned. This student was the latest victim—and she had seen the culprit!

The student stirred. His eyes fluttered open, and he coughed up blood.

"Hang on, son. An ambulance is on the way," a policeman said.

"I'm okay," the boy gasped.

"No, you're not. You're hurt. Don't move

. . . just tell us what happened. Can you identify your assailant?"

"I . . . no. I didn't see him," the boy said.

What! That was impossible, Nancy knew. The beating he had received must have lasted several minutes. How could he not have seen his attacker in that time?

"Are you sure?" the policeman asked. "Anything you can tell us will help."

"Sorry, I . . . I didn't see his face," the student insisted.

He was lying! But why?

Nancy stepped forward. "Excuse me. I saw the man. I was standing in the parking lot when he ran from the building. He nearly ran me down with his car."

Instantly she was surrounded by policemen. She gave her statement slowly and carefully. Her only regret was that she couldn't describe the man's face, only his approximate height and weight. That was all she had been able to see in the split second it had taken him to sprint from the dorm to his car.

When she was finished, the policemen turned to the student who had phoned them. He had heard the beating taking place and called from his room.

Nancy stayed until the ambulance arrived. As the student was wheeled away on a gurney, she heard him murmuring, "Please don't tell my parents! Please don't call them!"

There wasn't much hope of that, she knew. But why did he want his parents kept in the dark? Was he afraid they would be angry at him? Maybe he was just delirious. She didn't know.

"That was one crazy night you had!" George said the next morning.

Nancy pushed her scrambled eggs around her plate. "No kidding! Crazy and strange. I feel lucky to be here."

"Too bad that student wasn't as lucky as you." Bess shuddered. "Honestly, Nancy, I don't know how you could stand to look at him."

"I'm not sure, either."

That was the truth. At the time, the sight of his battered face hadn't bothered her. When she pictured it now, though, in the cold light of day, she felt sick.

"Well, at least it's over," George said, squeezing her hand.

"Not quite. This morning I remembered some details about the Camaro. It had smoked windows and custom hubcaps . . . you know, the ones that look like wire wheels? I should add that to my statement."

"What about the practical joker case?"

"I'll get back to it right after I visit the police station."

Outside, the air was warmer than it had been during the previous few days. The sun was bright.

Nancy had to step around the puddles in the sidewalks as she strolled across the campus toward the police station.

As she walked, her thoughts returned to Ned and their argument the night before. She couldn't blame him for sticking by Mike, but she couldn't understand it, either. How could he ignore something as obvious as the evidence in Mike's room? To her, that was like ignoring a Detour sign on a highway. It was foolish and dangerous—and it didn't make sense!

Her thoughts vanished, though, as she drew near the administration building. A demonstration was going on outside it—Tom Stafford and his crew again! What were they protesting this time? she wondered. The budget for the P.E. department again?

No. This time the campaign was a lot more serious, she saw. Their signs read "End Illegal Payments to Emerson Athletes!" and "No More Bucks for Burnett's Bribes!"

As she walked up, Nancy heard a reporter from the school newspaper quizzing Tom. ". . . so can you prove these charges?"

The student council president avoided a direct answer. "We're forcing the issue into the open. Pat Burnett must come clean!"

"You *don't* have proof, then," the reporter said knowingly.

"Look, it's common knowledge that illegal salaries are paid to college athletes," Tom said. "If you want hard evidence, then . . . then talk to *her!*" He pointed a finger at Nancy.

"Me!"

"She knows all about the under-the-table pay-offs to the basketball team!"

"Is that true?" the reporter asked, turning to her.

"Of course not! Don't be ridiculous," Nancy said indignantly.

"Well, what about your boyfriend and his pals? They live like kings! Where do you suppose they get the money?" Tom accused.

"What money? They don't seem rich to me."

"Oh, come on. Look at their parties . . . their cars . . . their clothes!"

Nancy folded her arms. "I'm sorry, but I don't know what you're talking about."

"No? Then tell me this—how do you think a small school like Emerson manages to recruit top talent like Mike O'Shea? By magic?"

"I don't know about Mike, but I know that Ned Nickerson plays basketball here because he admires and respects his coach."

"Give me a break! Pat Burnett's good, but he's not the best."

"So what?"

"Nickerson could play anywhere he wants to! But he doesn't. He plays for Emerson . . . and that's because he's paid!"

"You're crazy!"

Nancy was furious. How dare he suggest something like that. It was outrageous! He obviously didn't know Ned Nickerson as well as he thought he did!

Or did he? Suddenly Nancy remembered the bracelet she was wearing. It was lovely . . . silver . . . and expensive. Not only that, it wasn't the sort of gift that Ned usually gave her. Where *had* he gotten the money for the bracelet?

Something else fell into place, too: the flashy way in which Mike, Andy, and Craig had dressed at the party. Nancy knew they couldn't afford the stuff they had worn—they were all scholarship students! She had checked!

She tried to keep her expression natural, but the reporter was eyeing her with interest. "You don't know anything about illegal payments, then?" she asked.

"I . . . uh . . ."

"Sure she does. She doesn't want to admit it, that's all."

"That's not true! Believe me, if I had evidence I'd give it to you. But I don't. Now if you'll excuse me, I have things to do."

She sure did! As soon as she'd been to the police station, she'd find Ned right away! She had to ask him about Tom Stafford's accusation. Was it true?

And were illegal payments the reason he didn't want her to investigate Mike?

* * *

The sports complex was even larger inside than Nancy had thought. It would be hard to find Ned here, she knew, but she had no choice. He wasn't answering his phone, he wasn't at the library, and all his classes were in the afternoon. This was the only place left.

One by one, she checked the weight room, the pool, the squash courts. He wasn't in any of them. She checked the indoor track, but he wasn't there, either. Finally, she began to ask people if they had seen him. No one had.

She was ready to give up. There was one more possibility, though, she remembered—the complex's lowest level. She could try that.

Down the stairs she went to an empty white hallway. Machinery hummed behind several doors —the heating system, probably. There wasn't much chance that she would find him here, she realized. She turned . . .

. . . and stopped. Faintly she heard the *crack crack crack* of pistol shots. There was a rifle range nearby! Curious, she walked until she found its door. A small, square window was set into it, and she peered through.

Just then the door opened. A hand grabbed her by the arm, pulled her inside, and spun her around. Before she could scream, the warm barrel of a pistol was pressed against her neck!

Chapter

Seven

"SNOOPING AGAIN, NANCY?"

She knew that voice! Wrenching herself free, she whirled around in anger.

"Ray Ungar! Are you crazy? Don't you know that's dangerous?"

The former Wildcat looked hurt. "Hey, don't get steamed. I was only kidding. Anyway, the gun's not loaded . . . see?"

He held it out. The cartridge clip was missing, Nancy noticed. But that didn't make her feel better. Pistols were not weapons with which to joke around.

"I ought to report you to whoever's in charge of this range," she growled, straightening her shirt.

Ray's high, thin voice rose to a whine. "You won't rat on me, will you?"

"Why shouldn't I?"

"Ever since Burnett threw me off the basketball team, this is the only fun I have left."

"That doesn't give you the right to point your gun at another human being!"

"*Okay.* Excuse *me!* I won't do it again."

Nancy relaxed a little, but only a little. She wasn't comfortable around Ray. Who could be, when he acted so weird? In fact, if it weren't for Mike, she would gladly have put him at the top of her list of suspects!

Casually she glanced at the paper target on top of one of the firing stations. Its bullseye was shot out.

"That yours?" she asked.

"Yeah. Pretty good, huh? I've been shooting most of my life."

"Hmmm. . . . Listen, Ray, I'm looking for Ned. Have you seen him?"

Ray's face darkened. "Mr. Wonderful? No, I haven't seen him. Why don't you check the trophy case upstairs?"

"What! Why?"

"'Cause Burnett's got him on such a pedestal, he probably forgot and stuck him in there with all the other stuff."

Nancy stared at him. Was that supposed to be funny? Whether it was or not, she was getting out of there. She had heard enough. With a mumbled "See you," she turned and walked out.

She never did find Ned. When she got back to the dorm room, however, Bess informed her that Coach Burnett had called.

"Guess what? Tonight's game against Haviland University is away, and the coach gave us permission to ride on the team bus! Isn't that fantastic?"

Tremendous, Nancy thought sarcastically. It was going to be a barrel of laughs. How could she enjoy the ride with Tom Stafford's accusation ringing in her ears? Was it true? She was going to have to confront Ned with it sometime—and that would hurt both of them.

"Fantastic," Nancy replied dully.

At 4:30 that afternoon, Nancy, Bess, and George walked to the sports complex's parking lot. Bess was bubbling with enthusiasm. She was wearing a snazzy shirtdress under her coat and had bought a ten-foot-long, purple-and-orange Emerson scarf just for the occasion.

Aside from her jacket, Nancy was wearing boots, jeans, and a black cashmere sweater. She wasn't feeling very festive.

Most of the players had already arrived. Ned was there, his gym bag at his feet. He nodded as Nancy walked up but said nothing until Howie Little joined them. "Hey, Socks," Ned said.

"Socks?" Nancy asked.

"They call me that on account of the lucky pair I wear during games."

Nancy recalled seeing Howie's oddly colored socks two nights before. She was surprised to learn that he was superstitious.

"Hey, I've got the highest scoring average in the division. The best foul-shot percentage, too," he explained. "I'd say I'm entitled to wear any kind of socks I want to!"

"I guess you are!" Nancy laughed.

A minute later, the team manager told everyone to get on the bus.

"Won't Coach Burnett be riding with us?" Nancy asked as she climbed aboard.

Ned shook his head. "He rides to games with the assistant coaches."

"What about Mike? I don't see him, either."

"He's driving to Haviland by himself," Ned said carefully. "He . . . he told me that he needs some time to think."

About what? Nancy wondered. His next practical joke? Where to spend his money?

She decided not to sit with Ned. The only topic she wanted to discuss was the illegal payments, but this wasn't the right time, she knew. Instead, she sat with George in the seat right behind the driver.

The door closed with a hiss, and a second later they were off. It was a two-hour drive to Haviland. Nancy wondered how she would stand it. Her doubts about Ned were making her so unhappy that she could hardly sit still.

Fortunately, George didn't notice her anguish. Her friend was excited about the upcoming game. She knew a lot about basketball and filled the time by explaining the game's fine points.

". . . so you see, just before the final buzzer the losing team will commit a foul on purpose. That way they can—"

Her lecture was interrupted by a cry of rage from the back of the bus. Twisting around, Nancy tried to see what was happening.

It was Howie. The center was squatting in the aisle, emptying his gym bag onto the floor. "I don't believe it. I just don't believe it!" he said over and over.

"What happened?" Ned shouted to him.

"Some bozo stole my lucky socks outta my bag!"

An angry murmur swept through the bus. The practical joker had struck again! Was the Wildcats' luck ever going to change?

Just then, George touched her arm. "Nancy, look . . . that Camaro! Isn't that like the one you saw last night?"

Nancy turned to the left and looked out her window. A Camaro was cruising next to the bus in the fastest lane of the four-lane highway. It was black. It had smoked windows. Its hubcaps were flashing, exactly like—

In a flash, she realized that it wasn't *like* the killer Camaro—it *was* the killer Camaro! What was it doing here?

As she watched, horrified, the car moved into position alongside the bus's front wheel. Then its window powered down. A gun barrel appeared. There was a burst of flame, followed by a loud pop and a deafening hiss.

The front of the bus began to shudder wildly. The tire was out! The driver gave a panicky cry and stomped on the brake. In no time the bus skidded to the right, swinging across two entire lanes of the highway and narrowly missing the other traffic.

A loud screech came next. Screams and shouts filled the air as the bus started to tip over!

Chapter

Eight

THEY WERE DONE for, Nancy was certain of it! She braced for the impact, gripping her armrests tightly.

At the last second, however, the driver swung the wheel in the direction of the skid. The bus teetered crazily but slid to a halt without overturning.

Pandemonium broke loose. Amid the commotion, Nancy heard Ned shout, "Stay calm! Stay in your seats! Is everyone okay?"

A quick survey showed that no one was injured. Nerves were frayed, though, and it took several minutes for everyone to calm down enough to stop yelling.

Nancy checked the driver. He was unhurt but badly shaken.

"It's my fault," he said. "I shouldn't have hit the brakes."

"Don't worry about it. Everything turned out all right," she told him.

"Everything except the tire. What a time to have a blowout!"

Didn't he know that the tire had been shot out? Obviously not. Nancy wondered whether to tell him, but decided against it. What good would it do? The Camaro was gone, and spreading the story would only make the players more upset than they were already.

The driver used an emergency roadside phone to call for another bus. It arrived an hour later, and the team transferred into it. When they reached the Haviland gym it was just minutes before the game was due to start.

"Those guys are really shaken up," Bess said as the girls took their seats in the bleachers. She had been sitting in the back of the bus with cute Craig Watson and looked pretty shaken herself. "Do you think they'll win?"

"Let's hope so," Nancy said.

George added, "If they don't, it's goodbye playoffs!"

At first, the game looked like a rout. Emerson ran fast and hard, and quickly built a twenty-five point lead. The trouble came in the second half.

With just ten minutes to go, the Wildcats began to slip. Scoring opportunities went unnoticed. Foul shots missed. In no time, their lead faded to just twelve points.

Was it the shock of the near-disaster finally catching up with them? Nancy wondered. Probably. She cheered loudly, but her mind wasn't really on the game. Instead, she was brooding about the black Camaro. First it had turned up at the scene of an assault, and then it had been used to shoot out the bus's tire!

In her mind, that could mean only one thing: The beatings and the practical jokes against the team were connected. But how? And why? She had no idea.

When the final buzzer sounded, Emerson had won the game by nine points.

On the return trip Nancy reversed two of the seats so that she, George, Bess, and Ned could sit together. Softly, so that the other team members wouldn't hear, they discussed the case. Ned was shocked when he heard about the Camaro and its part in the accident.

"Nancy, you should have called the police!" he said.

"There wasn't any point. I missed the license number again. Anyway, why delay the trip even more by bringing in the cops? We almost missed the start of the game as it was!"

"True."

Nancy slumped in her seat. "The real issue is that Camaro driver. Why would someone who likes to beat up people also pull a practical joke? It doesn't make sense."

"Some practical joke," Bess muttered. "That bullet almost got us killed!"

"Not true. Think about it . . . it wasn't the shot that almost spilled the bus, but the way the driver hit the brakes."

"Oh, sure. If that Camaro guy wasn't trying to kill us, then what was he trying to do?"

"Slow us down," Nancy explained. "He wanted the team to arrive late . . . maybe even late enough to make them forfeit the game."

"Hmmm . . ."

George was puzzled about something else. "I don't understand . . . why do you think it's weird that the same guy is responsible for both the pranks and the assaults?"

"Yeah, it makes perfect sense to me," Ned agreed.

Nancy shook her head. "Beating people up and playing jokes on them are two different things. One involves direct physical contact, while the other involves watching from a distance."

"But the Camaro definitely ties the two cases together," Ned pointed out.

"You're right, it does."

"Who do you think was driving it?" George asked next.

Nancy shrugged. "That's the big question. I don't know."

Silence. For several minutes the foursome sifted the clues in their minds. For her part, Nancy felt that one suspect stood out more than any other—Mike O'Shea. He had not been with the team when the tire was shot. There was also the effigy material in his room. Should she voice her suspicion? She knew how Ned would react, but that was not the reason she kept quiet.

The reason was that she now had another strong suspect—Ray Ungar. That morning at the rifle range she had learned that he was a crack marksman. Could he have been the one who shot out the bus's tire? Unless he had a rock-solid alibi, it was possible, she knew.

It was George who suggested the third suspect. "I think it's that creep Tom Stafford," she said forcefully.

"Tom! Why him?" Ned asked.

"Well, he wants the trustees to cut the P.E. department's budget, right?"

"Uh-huh."

"There you go! He's sabotaging the Wildcats' season in order to give the trustees an excuse to zap the funding."

"I don't know . . . that sounds too elaborate," Ned said doubtfully.

"Come on, the guy's a fanatic! He'd do anything to further his cause!"

George had a point, Nancy had to admit. Tom

was an idealist, and idealists sometimes got carried away. At any rate, they had a motive for Tom—more than she could say about Mike!

"I think you have it wrong, George," Bess declared. "I think the joker is that weirdo Ray Ungar that Nancy told us about."

"Oh? Why?"

"Because he hates the Wildcats. Or at least Coach Burnett. I say he's playing the pranks as revenge for being kicked off the team."

Nodding, Nancy filled them in on her encounter with Ray in the rifle range.

"That clinches it as far as I'm concerned," Ned said grimly. "Ray's our man. All we have to do is find out whether he has an alibi for this afternoon and if he drives a Camaro."

"Forget it. It's not going to be that easy," Nancy objected. "Naturally, the joker's going to have an alibi. And as for the Camaro . . . he'd be a fool to drive it around openly."

"And our practical joker is no fool," George added.

"I suppose you're right."

Another silence fell. Where did they go from here? Nancy wondered. Tom, Ray, Mike—any of them could be the practical joker. Each had points in his favor, yet there wasn't enough evidence to pin down any of them.

Once again they were at a dead end. She felt more frustrated than ever. The bigger this case grew, the harder it seemed to be to crack. Whoever he was, this practical joker had earned her respect: With one possible exception, he had pulled off all his crimes without leaving any clues.

Back at Emerson, the young detective said an awkward goodnight to Ned and started back to the dorm with her friends. The three walked in silence. Their mood was gloomy.

Finally, Bess spoke. "This is awful. It seems like there's no way to catch this guy. You've seen him, though, right?"

"Last night in the parking lot," George said, "didn't you get any idea about who he might be?"

Nancy sighed. "No, and believe me, I've thought about it plenty. All I could tell was that the guy is tall and thin. That description could fit lots of people."

"Like Tom."

"Or Ray."

"Or Mike," Nancy concluded.

Not even seeing the practical joker in the flesh had done any good! Maybe Bess was right, Nancy thought darkly. Maybe there wasn't any way to catch him at all!

A few minutes later, the trio rounded the corner of a large, windowless brick building. From the tall smokestack rising above it, Nancy guessed that it was the college's central heating plant.

Suddenly George grabbed Nancy's arm. "Nancy, look . . . over there by that fence! It's the Camaro!"

Chapter

Nine

NANCY'S HEART BEGAN to race. George was right! To one side a short drive widened into a small shipping yard. On the yard's far side, parked near a snow fence, was the Camaro!

There was no question that it was the one. It had the same smoked windows and the same custom hubcaps.

"I don't believe it! What a break!" Nancy nearly shouted. "I'm going over there to get its license number."

Bess whitened. "But, Nan, that guy could be somewhere around here!"

"I'll be careful."

As she started toward it, however, the car's

headlights blazed on. Its engine roared to life. The driver was still inside—the dark windows had hidden him from view!

Nancy watched in horror as the car leapt forward with a screech. He was going to get away! She had to stop him!

She glanced around wildly. At the top of the entrance drive was a pyramid of steel drums. She ran toward them, her hair flying. When she reached them she pushed with all her might, praying that they were empty.

They were. The top three drums tumbled over and began to roll slowly. Trapped, the Camaro skidded to a stop. Smoke spun from its rear tires as it flew backward. In no time it came to a stop near the open loading-bay door that led into the heating plant. What was he doing?

The driver's door swung open. For a brief instant his tall, thin figure was silhouetted in the plant's doorway. Then he disappeared inside.

"Quick! He's getting away! Let's go after him!" Nancy shouted.

George caught her at the entrance. "Nancy, don't you think we should just get the license number and call the police?"

"Yes, let the cops handle it," Bess agreed as she ran up.

"No way! Don't you see? This is probably the only entrance to the building—we can trap him inside! Come on, you guys!"

Inside, Nancy tugged on the chain to the overhead door. It wouldn't budge.

"Oh no! We're going to have to hunt him down! George, you and Bess go around to the right. I'll go the other way."

"But, Nancy—!"

"Be careful. He probably has his gun."

Nancy didn't give them time to object. Quick as a flash she darted to the left, making her way around the side of a massive steam turbine, the noise from which was deafening.

The corridor ahead of her was empty. She crept forward warily, prepared to throw herself to the floor at any second. She reached the corridor's end without a problem, though. Trembling slightly, she peered around the corner.

The corridor jogged right for ten feet, then left again. Nancy took the double corner cautiously, then crept forward once more. Tension mounted inside her. Somewhere ahead was the practical joker. Was it Mike? Ray? Tom? Whoever he was, he was very likely armed and dangerous!

Finally, she reached the last corner. She was at the back of the heating plant, she knew. With George and Bess coming down the other side, that meant that the joker was trapped. Taking a deep breath to calm herself, she flattened herself against a wire mesh cage and risked a peek.

George and Bess were coming toward her, looks of fear on their faces.

Nancy stepped around the corner with a cry. "Hey! Where did he go?"

Her friends jumped. Bess looked ready to faint. "Aaargh! Don't do that! You nearly scared me to death, Nancy!"

"Sorry. I was sure we had him trapped back here. What happened?"

George pointed. "Look!"

Off to their left, a large tunnel angled down and away from the heating plant. Attached to its walls were dozens of pipes and ducts. So! There *was* another way out!

"What is that?" Bess asked. "What are all those pipes?"

Nancy started toward the opening. "They hold the electrical cables, I'll bet. The ducts probably carry leftover steam from the turbines."

"Carry it where?"

"To the other buildings, for heat."

George's eyes bugged out. "Nancy, are you saying there's a maze of tunnels under the campus?"

"I wouldn't doubt it. And that's where the joker went. Come on!"

The tunnel was suffocatingly hot. Pursuing the joker here was highly dangerous, Nancy knew, but she was determined to catch him. He had hurt too many people in too many ways to let him escape now that they had him!

On and on they jogged. The tunnel twisted and

turned, and they had to peer around every corner in case the joker lay ahead. Nancy was worried. Their caution was slowing them down. He might escape.

Finally, they came to a fork. Nancy looked both ways but saw no one in the dim light. Which way had he gone?

"Should we split up?" George asked.

"No, I may need your help when we catch him." Nancy slipped off her jacket.

Bess shucked off her coat, too. "I say we split—period! Let's find the fastest way out of here. I'm dying of the heat!"

Nancy wiped her forehead. "The joker's probably thinking that way, too. The question is, which is the shortest way out?"

They took the right branch. Two turns and a fifty-yard stretch later, they found themselves in a large basement. The word *Jenkins* was painted on the wall.

"This is one of the dormitories!" Nancy said. "Ned lived here before he joined his fraternity. Come on!"

Together they ran up a flight of stairs, down a brightly lit hallway, and out a door. They were outside again! Quickly Nancy looked around, searching for familiar landmarks.

"There! The smokestack!" she shouted. "Let's go!"

It took less than a minute to return to the

heating plant, but by then it was too late. As they rounded the corner of the building and spotted the shipping yard, Nancy let out a howl of pent-up rage.

The Camaro was gone!

"It's my fault. I should have sent one of you back for the police. Or even for the license number," Nancy said.

It was the next morning. Nancy, Bess, and George were eating breakfast in a big, airy dining hall.

"Don't kick yourself too hard," George advised her. "It was a tense situation, and you did what you thought best."

"Yes, but look where it got us . . . nowhere! Now we're back to square one." Nancy groaned.

"Not exactly," Bess interrupted.

"What do you mean?" Nancy asked, looking over at her blond friend.

Until now, Bess's nose had been buried in the most recent issue of the student newspaper. She had picked it up on their way into the dining hall and had hardly looked up since.

"I've just eliminated one of our suspects," she announced.

"You're kidding! How?"

"By reading this paper. See? This article says that Tom Stafford led a debate against Fielding College last night."

"So?" George demanded.

"The debate began at five P.M., the same time that the bus's tire was shot!"

"Therefore, Tom couldn't have done it," Nancy concluded.

"Right!"

"Wait a minute," George objected. "What about his loyal followers . . . couldn't one of them have done it?"

Nancy considered that idea. "No, I don't think so. Remember seeing them outside the sports complex? They weren't as fanatical as Tom."

"I think Tom's the only one crazy enough to do something like that."

"How would you know, Bess? You've never even seen him!" George pointed out.

"True, but so what? Admit it, George—you're just disappointed that your favorite suspect is out of the running."

George grinned. "Well, maybe I am."

"I'd better tell Ned about this," Nancy said, lifting her jacket from the back of her chair and pulling it on.

George nodded. "Good idea. A healthy one, too." She pushed aside her tray with a grimace. "I hate to say it, but the food here is terrible!"

"You said it," Bess agreed. "Those pancakes taste like rubber."

Nancy had barely touched her breakfast. How could she eat when everything was such a mess? She was making little progress with the case, and as for her relationship with Ned—that seemed to be going backward!

Outside, the sky was gray and threatening. The forecast was for snow, and it appeared to be only a matter of time before the storm began. Nancy hurried across the campus, her head down, her spirits very low.

Were things between her and her boyfriend ever going to return to normal? When they'd disagreed over Mike it had torn her apart, and now there was something worse: the possibility that Ned was accepting cash to play for Emerson.

Nancy felt angry whenever she thought about that. Ned—*her* Ned—taking bribes? It was ridiculous! And yet, why keep her from investigating Mike? Why work against her when solving the case would help his team? There was also the silver bracelet. Nancy had taken it off the day before and hidden it away. Looking at it made her very uncomfortable.

She couldn't continue living with these ugly suspicions, she knew. She had to talk to him. She had to find out the truth!

Ned was at the sports complex studying a videotape of the Haviland game. Nancy slipped into the viewing room quietly. For a moment she studied *him*. In his jeans and rust-colored crewneck sweater, he looked as adorable as ever. His brow was furrowed in concentration.

"Admiring yourself again, Nickerson?" she

said. She tried for a teasing tone, but the words came out all wrong.

Ned turned. "Oh, it's you."

"I thought you'd like to know that I've ruled out Tom Stafford as a suspect," she said quickly.

"Great," he nodded. "That leaves only Ray Ungar, right?"

"Uh . . ."

Ned's dark eyes narrowed. His square-cut face grew hard. "Don't bother to say it, Nancy. I can read it in your expression. You still think Mike is guilty."

"Ned, what if he *is!* Has it ever occurred to you that you might be wrong?"

"Sure it has. But I'm not changing my position. I know Mike. If he's mixed up in anything funny, then sooner or later he'll come clean."

"Oh, Ned."

This wasn't going at all the way she had hoped it would. Instead of mending fences they were getting ready for another argument.

"Look," Nancy said. "Let's not talk about that. There's something else I want to discuss with you. It's about—"

She never finished her sentence. Just then her eyes shifted to the TV screen, where the tape of the Haviland game was still playing.

"Ned, stop the tape!" she shouted. "I think I just spotted the practical joker!"

Chapter

Ten

NED, I'M SERIOUS. Stop the tape and rerun it," Nancy repeated.

Ned was looking at her strangely, but the urgency in her voice was too powerful to ignore. Reaching over, he pressed several buttons on the VCR. The tape stopped and began to rewind.

"How far?" he asked.

"Just a couple of feet," she said. She stepped close to the screen as the tape started again. "Okay, right here . . . watch what happens to the camera!"

The scene was a play toward the end of the game's first half. The Emerson players brought the ball down court, dribbling and passing with deadly skill. Ned then set a classic "pick," blocking the Haviland player guarding Mike. Mike drove to the basket and scored two points.

"What's so special about that?" Ned wanted to know. "All that's happening is—"

"*There!*" Nancy jabbed the freeze-frame button. "It's not the play, it's what happens when it's over . . . see? Somebody knocks the camera and it picks up part of the audience."

"Yes, but—"

"Look closely. Who's that?" Nancy pointed to a blurry but recognizable figure.

"Ray Ungar!" Ned gasped. His astonishment faded quickly, though. "I don't get it, Nancy. What does this prove?"

Nancy unzipped her jacket and dropped into the chair next to Ned's. "Didn't you tell me that Ray never goes to Wildcat games?"

"Yes. He once swore he'd never attend another one as long as he lives."

"Yet there he is among the spectators! Don't you find that odd?"

Understanding flashed in Ned's eyes. "It was a deliberate deception, you mean? We were told we wouldn't see him, therefore we didn't?"

"Right! And it allowed Ray to do what he really wanted to do—sit in the bleachers and enjoy the effects of his practical jokes!"

Beaming, Ned leapt up and crushed her in a

joyful hug. "Nancy, you've done it again! Now Mike is in the clear!"

It felt wonderful to have Ned's arms around her again. As she hugged him back, though, something nagged at the back of her mind. After a minute, she pulled away.

"Ned, play it over again, will you?"

"Sure thing. Wait until everyone sees this!"

Nancy shook her head as the scene unfolded once more. The camera focused on Ray for only a second or two, but it was long enough for her to realize that she had been wrong.

"I'm sorry, Ned, but it looks to me like Ray is cheering Mike's basket."

Ned's face fell. "What are you saying?"

"That Ray can't be the practical joker. If he were, then why would he cheer for the Wildcats?"

"But, Nancy, you just said—"

"I know. I spoke too soon."

They reran the tape several more times, but each viewing only reinforced Nancy's belief that her theory was incorrect. Why Ray was supporting Emerson she didn't know, but he was no longer her prime suspect.

Ned reacted angrily. "I don't believe this! One minute you're telling me Mike is okay, and the next you're accusing him again!"

"I can't help it. Facts are facts."

"What *facts*? That tape doesn't clear Ray."

Not totally, she had to agree. It was possible—

just possible—that even though he was cheering for Emerson he was still responsible for the pranks. But Nancy didn't think so.

"Ned, Ray isn't the practical joker. It's just common sense," she stated.

"Oh, sure. He dumps on the team, even holds a pistol to your head, and you call it common sense? Wake up, Nancy! Ray's crazy! Can't you see that?"

"Maybe, but that doesn't make him guilty."

"It doesn't make him look very innocent, either."

"Ned, all we have against Ray are suspicions. With Mike we have hard evidence!"

"That box of packing chips?" Ned snorted. "That's not enough for me. If you're going to change my mind, you'll have to show me more."

Furious, Nancy rose from her chair. All at once she was fed up with Ned's attitude. Why did he have to be so pig-headed? Why did he have to fight her this way? She clenched her fists.

"All right, Nickerson. It's evidence you want? Then evidence you'll get!" She was trembling. "And don't try to stop me!"

"Nancy, what are you planning?"

"Why should I tell you?" she cried.

"I don't want you to get hurt."

She laughed bitterly. "Ha! I don't think you care about me at all!"

With that, she whirled around and stormed from the room.

Nancy was still seething that night as she stood outside the sports complex. Over and over again she pictured Ned's stubborn expression and heard his hostile words. I'll show him, she thought.

Snow was swirling around her, but she didn't go inside. Instead, she stood in the shadows, watching the building's entrance. Once in a while she stamped her feet or rubbed her arms.

She checked her watch. The illuminated dial read 11:35 P.M. There was still time, she knew, but she was mildly worried. The building would close for the night in twenty-five minutes.

Finally, she got her chance. Through the glass entrance doors she saw the security guard leave his desk. Quickly she ran up and slipped inside. She had done it! She had gotten in without signing the guest register!

Walking casually, she made her way to the girls' locker room, entered a toilet stall, locked the door, stood on the seat . . . and waited.

Midnight arrived. As it did, the security guards swept through the building to make sure it was empty. Because they were male, Nancy guessed that they would give the girls' locker room only a superficial glance. She was right. No one bothered to check the stall in which she was hidden, even though its door was shut and locked.

The lights went out. Nancy waited ten minutes, then moved. Her destination lay down a side hall, away from the main thoroughfares, so she didn't have to worry much about running into one of the security guards. Along a row of administrative offices she did have to dart past one lighted doorway, though. Who would still be working at this hour? she wondered briefly. The next moment she forgot her question and continued on.

The basketball team's locker room was open, she found. Slipping inside, she took her car flashlight from her jacket and flipped it on. One by one, she scanned the names taped to the face of each locker until she came to the one she wanted.

Michael O'Shea.

Fortunately, Mike kept an ordinary padlock on his locker. Nancy could crack simple combination locks with no problem, but key types were easier. She drew her lockpick from her pocket and quietly went to work.

She had it open in less than a minute. Mike had the usual assortment of junk in his locker: towels, uniform, sneakers, hand weights, knee brace, ointments, and a sports magazine. He also had an envelope that contained two thousand dollars in twenty-dollar bills, and a list of Emerson's opponents. Beside each one was a negative number: -10, -14, -6, -17. . . .

What did the numbers mean? Nancy hadn't the slightest idea. She was positive about one thing, though: Mike was up to no good!

Suddenly she froze. Footsteps were coming down the hall!

She had to hide. Glancing around quickly, she noticed several old, unused locker sections against one wall. Should she slip into one of those? No, she decided. It would be a tight squeeze and they might not open from the inside. Where then? The showers?

She spotted a better place—the sauna! Darting across the room, she pulled open its wooden door and zipped inside. Through the narrow window in the door, she saw the lights in the locker room come on.

Nancy shrank back against an interior wall, her heart racing. Too late, she realized that she had forgotten to shut Mike's locker! Oh, well. There was nothing she could do about that now. If she was lucky the security guard—or whoever—would think that Mike himself had forgotten to close it. Swallowing hard, she held still and listened.

Outside, there was silence. Then some bumping and scraping began. It sounded as if equipment was being moved around, but she couldn't be sure. Who was it? A janitor mopping floors? Nancy remained motionless as several loud clunks sounded right outside the sauna door.

Finally, after what seemed like hours, there was

silence again. The window in the sauna's door went dark, indicating that the locker room lights had been turned off.

Relieved, Nancy waited for a minute, then went to the sauna door to leave. It wouldn't budge. She pushed harder, but still the door wouldn't open. It was blocked from the outside!

Not only that, Nancy realized—the sauna was beginning to get warm! Whoever it was had cranked up the thermostat. She was trapped!

Chapter

Eleven

SLOWLY THE TEMPERATURE climbed. How hot could one of these saunas get? Nancy wondered. 110°? 120°? Hotter?

It didn't matter, really. Whoever had blocked her in had probably cranked it up as high as it would go. The point was, how long could she continue to function under such high temperatures? Twenty minutes? Half an hour?

Her assailant had undoubtedly jammed the timer, too, she knew.

Nancy removed her jacket. Already she could feel a drop of sweat trickling down her back. At least she still had her flashlight! Flicking it on, she looked around.

The sauna contained nothing more than a heating unit bolted to the wall, a wooden floor, and a bench made of wooden slats. That was it. No tools. No loose objects. Nothing she could use to help pry or batter her way out.

She examined the door. Its hinges were on the outside. She pushed against it once more. No good! The door swung outward an inch, but that was all. What was on the other side, anyway? An elephant?

No, she realized—the unused lockers! Two or more sections had been pushed across the floor and fitted sideways against the door. That explained the bumps and scrapes she had heard. Great. Now how was she going to get out?

Calmly at first, then with mounting concern, she examined the possibilities.

Screaming? The sound of her voice had to travel through two doors, down a side hallway, down a main hallway, and then maybe—just maybe—a guard would eventually hear it. Forget it, she told herself. Better to conserve energy.

Bess and George? She had told them where she was going, naturally, but how long would it take them to realize that something had gone wrong? Until one o'clock? Two o'clock? That was no use! She could be dead by then!

No, she would have to get herself out of this. But how?

The air around her was growing very hot. To help herself stay cool, Nancy took off her boots, jeans, and sweater. That helped, but not too much. She was sweating heavily, and the hot air was burning her lungs.

How much longer before she got dizzy? she wondered. Would her vision begin to blur? What then?

Stop it! Get yourself out of here! her mind screamed.

Going to the door again, she pushed it hard. It wouldn't budge! She hammered at it with her hands, but that was even more futile than pushing. The exertion was making her sweat more, too.

She sat down on the bench and tried to think. Impossibly, the air seemed to grow hotter still. She was turning into roast detective—and fast!

Ned. This was all his fault, she told herself bitterly. If he hadn't been so stubborn, then she wouldn't have had to gather evidence by such desperate means. Well, he was going to be sorry! When they found her body here in the morning (cooked medium-well) he was going to—

Get out! Get out! Get out! Once again, she willed herself into action, snatching up her flashlight, only to drop it again. It was burning hot! How was she going to see anything now? If only there was a light—

The overhead light, of course! Why hadn't she thought of that sooner! Using her shirt as insulation, she picked up the flashlight and looked around. Yes, there was the switch by the door! She flipped it on, and light flooded the sauna.

Now she needed something small and made of metal. Reaching into the pocket of her jeans, she brought out her silver pen. It was a gift from her father that she treasured, but right now that didn't matter. Saving her life was more important than saving the pen!

Carefully she wrapped her leather belt around one end of it. Then, standing on the bench, she held the pen in one hand and removed the overhead light bulb with the other, using her shirt to keep from burning her hand. The sauna went dark. Again and again she jabbed the pen upward until, at last, it plunged into the live socket!

Sparks showered around her. Nancy smelled smoke and gave a cry of triumph. There! She had shorted the circuit! Had she tripped the breaker that controlled the heating unit, too?

Stepping off the bench, she peered through the unit's vent. Inside, its heating coils slowly changed from white . . . to orange . . . to red . . . to nothing! Thank goodness! At least the sauna wasn't going to get any hotter.

It was still very hot, though. Not only that, her condition was deteriorating. She was dizzy. More than anything in the world she wanted to lie down and close her eyes. But she couldn't. She had to keep going!

Taking up her sweater and flashlight again, she went to the bench and again began to tug each of its slats. All were pegged securely in place, but one seemed a little loose. She tugged at it, fighting off dizziness, until it came free. Then, wasting no time, she used it to punch out the window in the door.

Cool air rushed in through the opening. Nancy nearly cried with relief. Pushing the slat through the opening, she used it as a lever. The locker outside didn't move at first, but then she caught a metal lip and the side closest to her lifted six inches into the air. She was unable to overturn the monster, but it *did* slide backward a bit. A few more tries, and she had worked it back an entire foot!

She tried the door. It opened farther, but not enough. Working with the slat, she levered and pushed, slowly moving the lockers backward. Finally, she opened the door wide enough to slip out!

But would she make it? In spite of the cool air now washing over her clammy skin, Nancy was exhausted. Her head ached, and bright spots of color were dancing before her eyes. Reeling, she groped for her clothes and boots. Did she have them in her hands? She wasn't sure. Never mind, she thought . . .

. . . just get out the door!

"Nancy, you shouldn't be up! You should be in bed, resting," Bess wailed.

Nancy didn't answer. Instead, she pulled a gray Emerson sweatshirt over her head and ran her fingers through her hair. She had things to do this morning. Important things—like confronting a certain Emerson forward named Mike O'Shea!

"Come on, Nancy, won't you sleep just a little bit longer?" Bess pleaded.

"Oh, leave her alone," said George, who was lying on her bed. "You know what that look on her face means. She's up, and that's it!"

"Well, all right. But why kill yourself when you don't have to?"

That was exactly the point, Nancy felt. She could have died in that sauna, and it had been totally unnecessary. The evidence in Mike's room should have convinced her. But no, like a fool she had listened to Ned.

Well, no more! Nancy Drew was not going to act like a wimp for one minute longer! She now had more than enough evidence to make a case against Mike, and that was exactly what she was going to do! As soon as she found her boots.

An hour later, a solid breakfast in her stomach, Nancy marched up to the front door of Omega Chi Epsilon. She was about to pull it open when a girl burst out—a short, snub-nosed brunette. It was Mike's girlfriend, she remembered.

"Excuse me," the girl said. She started to walk past Nancy, but then stopped. "Wait, aren't you Ned's girlfriend?"

"That's right. Nancy Drew."

"Hi. We met at the party the other night, remember? My name's Jan . . . Jan Teller."

"Yes, I remember." Nancy held out her hand.

Jan didn't look very happy, she noticed. Her eyes had circles under them, and she was glancing around nervously.

"Jan, I know this is a nosy question, but are you okay?" Nancy asked.

"Sure!" Jan said, trying to look cheerful. "I just—oh, who am I kidding? I'm not okay. I feel totally awful!"

"Is there anything I can do to help?"

"Thanks, but no. It's my boyfriend, Mike . . . you've met him, haven't you?"

Nancy nodded. Had she ever!

"He's been impossible lately," Jan continued. "Moody. Irritable. Sometimes he even disappears and won't tell me where he's been!"

"Maybe he's just tense because of the pressure on the Wildcats," Nancy suggested carefully.

"Oh, no . . . it's not that. Mike loves basketball! He's usually very happy during the season. I don't know what's going on, but whatever it is it's driving me crazy!"

You and me both, Nancy thought. Aloud, she said, "I'm sorry you're having problems. I hope you two can work them out."

"Yeah. Me, too," Jan said miserably. "The way things are going, though, I don't have much hope. Well, 'bye. I've got to run."

With that, she turned and walked away. Nancy felt sorry for her, yet she had a feeling that things were about to get even worse for Jan than they were already.

Mike was in the otherwise empty common room, sitting in an armchair. A chemistry textbook was open on his lap, but he didn't appear to be reading it.

"Mike?"

He looked up. "Nancy! Haven't seen much of you since you got to Emerson. How are you? Are you having a good time?"

Nancy felt herself tense. "I'd be having a much better one if I could get some answers to a few questions I have."

"Questions?"

"Yes. Such as, can you explain what *this* is all about?"

Reaching into her back pocket, she tossed a scrap of paper onto his textbook. It was the list of names and negative numbers from his locker. She had stuffed it into her pocket while running into the sauna the night before.

Mike's eyes narrowed. "Where did you get that?"

"You know where . . . from your locker. I saw the money there, too."

"There's no law against keeping money in a locker, is there?"

So, he was going to play it cool, was he? Nancy was disappointed. She had hoped to shock him into making a confession. Obviously, it was not going to be that easy.

She glared at him. "Don't try to kid me, Mike. I

know what you're up to. The only thing I don't know is why. Are you going to tell me, or shall I let the police drag it out of you?"

He crumpled the paper in his fist. "Police? What are you talking about? I haven't done anything wrong! Not a thing!"

"No? What about the box of packing chips in your room?"

For a split second, panic flashed across his face. "They . . . they're just junk."

"Just like the scraps of material mixed in with them?"

"You don't know what you're talking about!"

"I think I do. You've been playing practical jokes on your team, and some of them have been very dangerous, to say the least."

"That's not true!"

"Oh, no?"

Nancy crossed her arms. They were playing a bluffing game now, a game that she was winning. All she had to do was to keep wearing him down. Sooner or later he would confess.

"Tell me . . . why didn't you ride with the team to the Haviland game?" she demanded.

"That's no secret. I needed to be alone for a while."

"Alone to do what? To shoot out the bus's tire?"

He half rose from his chair. "Wait a minute! Are you suggesting—?"

"You know it."

"Well, you're wrong! Why would I do something like that?"

Nancy shrugged. "Fun? Money? You tell me. All I know is that you own a lot of things that most scholarship students don't . . . a gold watch . . . a black Camaro . . ."

"A *what!*"

"Where do you keep it, Mike? Do you drive it around a lot, or only when you go cruising for people to beat up?"

"You're out of your mind!"

He was on his feet now, pacing back and forth with a worried expression. She had him—Nancy was sure of it! It was only a matter of minutes before he made a full confession.

"Mike, why not tell me all about it?" she coaxed him gently. "It will be a lot easier that way, I promise."

"Nancy, I don't know where you got all these loony ideas, but you're totally wrong. I've never beaten up anyone in my life!"

A tremor of doubt rippled through her. Could he have some kind of split personality? Was it possible that he wasn't aware of all the things he had been doing?

"Mike, trust me. I'm not the only one who can see what's happening. Your teammates see it. So does Jan!"

"Jan? You've been talking to her?"

"Yes, and she's very worried about you. Please,

Mike . . . tell me everything, okay? Do it for Jan. Do it for yourself!"

A curious calm fell over him then. He rose to his full height, as if a great invisible burden was lifting from his shoulders. His voice grew strong and determined.

"Nancy, I want to thank you. You've made me see how stupid I've been."

"Then you'll tell me what all those negative numbers mean?" she asked triumphantly.

"I . . . no. They don't mean anything. Not anymore," he said.

Nancy felt her jaw drop. "But—"

"Listen, you don't have to worry about me. I've made a few mistakes, I guess, but I'm not the kind of person you think I am. Not by a long shot. Now, will you excuse me? I have some important business to take care of."

With that, he strode purposefully from the room. Nancy watched him go in shock. What was happening? Just when she thought she had turned him, he was walking out!

A minute later she was on her way back to the dorm, trying desperately to figure out how she had blown it. Had she pushed too hard? Not hard enough? Whatever it was, she had failed to get the confession she needed.

That wasn't good. The practical joker was still at large, and who could tell what kind of trouble he would make next?

Partway across campus, she stopped. Ahead of her, half a dozen police cars had pulled up outside a classroom building. What was going on? she wondered.

She walked up to a policeman. What he told her sent an icy chill down her spine. "It's another one of those assaults, miss . . . and this one looks especially bad!"

Chapter

Twelve

A FEELING OF horror swept through her. In no
time she remembered how Mike had hurried from
the fraternity common room. Was this the "important business" that he had insisted on attending
to?

It was possible. Ten minutes or more had passed
since she, too, had left the fraternity. Mike could
have done it in that time. Especially if he had been
driving a Camaro. It was harder to imagine the
police also arriving so quickly, but who could tell?
The way this case was going, Nancy was ready to
believe almost anything.

She had to get inside, Nancy decided. She felt

responsible for what had happened. If she had thought faster she might have stopped Mike. The assault might not have occurred.

The police had roped off the building's main entrance, so she walked instead to a door on one side. It was easy to find the scene of the assault: Policemen were everywhere, their radios crackling. In the middle of it all lay the student. A red emergency blanket was spread over him, but his face was visible. Nancy edged close . . . and gasped.

It was Captain Hook, the hunk she had seen talking on the phone!

With a jolt, she remembered how handsome she had found him that morning in the student bookstore. He didn't look very good now, though. His face was purple with bruises, and one of his eyes was swollen shut. He wasn't moving.

Nancy turned to a nearby policeman. "Is he going to be all right?" she asked.

"Hard to say," the officer shrugged. "He was worked over fairly hard."

"Is he conscious?"

"No, he's out."

Nancy turned away, then walked outside, feeling shaky. Maybe she should have taken Bess's advice and remained in bed, she thought. That wasn't realistic, though. Time was quickly running out. The final Emerson game was that night, and unless she put the practical joker out of action before then it was dead certain that he would stage one final prank, a prank that would be aimed at knocking Emerson out of the running for good.

That wouldn't be the end of it, either. Who could tell how long the beatings would continue? They might go on until each and every Emerson student had either been attacked or frightened away!

What should she do? As she walked toward the dorm, she turned over the possibilities. She couldn't go to the police, of course. She had evidence against Mike, but no positive proof.

Maybe she could get to him through Jan Teller, she thought. If she told Mike's girlfriend about the awful things he was doing, Jan might agree to talk to him, to ask him to turn himself in. But no, she decided, that plan had too many problems. It would take time, for one thing. For another, there was no guarantee that Mike would cooperate.

Ned? Help from her boyfriend was definitely out of the question, she knew. The new evidence from Mike's locker would not convince him of his co-captain's guilt. She was beginning to think that *nothing* would convince him of that!

Was that because he was guilty of taking illegal payments himself?

For the hundredth time, Nancy's thoughts returned to the awful possibility that the boy she loved was not the boy she thought he was. Would he even tell her the truth when she finally asked him? She didn't know. In a way, she felt like she didn't know anything anymore. Since this case had started, her world had turned upside down. Would she ever get it straightened out?

Nancy needed to sit down and think. Looking around, she spotted the library off to her right. She walked briskly toward it.

Inside, the building smelled of books and floor wax. Nancy walked to an area crammed with study cubicles, slipped into an empty one, and sat down. Mentally, she tried to sort through the pieces of the puzzle.

Suddenly a student working nearby caught her attention. Ray Ungar! What was he doing here? The library was the last place she ever expected to see him, especially on a Saturday!

Ray looked up and saw her watching him. Instantly, he scooped up his books and started to leave. Nancy blocked his exit.

"Ray, wait! You don't have to go."

"Why should I stay? So you can pry into my life some more?"

"I'm not prying into your life. I'm not doing anything to you at all."

"Sure," he snapped. "Tell me another one. You're just like everyone else. You think I'm funny . . . stupid Ray, Mr. Flunk-out!"

Nancy stared. What was he talking about? Why did he sound so bitter? "Ray, would you mind explaining this to me? I'm not trying to make fun of you. I'm trying to understand!"

He hesitated. At first Nancy thought he would go, but then he dropped his books on top of his desk with a clatter.

"All my life I've had trouble in school," Ray said. "Math, English, history . . . other kids learn that stuff easy, but not me. I have to work, and work hard, just to get C's!"

"That's not so unusual. Lots of kids have trouble in school."

"Yeah, well, that doesn't make it any easier for me. The only time I feel like somebody important is when I play basketball."

"I see. Is that why you hate Coach Burnett so much? Because he cut you from the team and took away your self-respect?"

Ray looked surprised. "I don't hate Coach! He *had* to cut me from the team. My grades were too low . . . that's the rules!"

"Wait a minute! Hold on . . ." Nancy touched her temples with her fingertips. "Am I hearing this right? You don't think Coach Burnett did anything wrong when he cut you?"

"No way."

"Then why do you claim to hate the team? Why did you swear you'd never go to another Wildcat game as long as you live?"

"Oh, that! I was just ticked off. I didn't mean what I said."

"So at the Haviland game, you really *were* cheering for Emerson?"

"How did you know I was there?"

"I saw you on a videotape," she explained. "Look, Ray, there's still something I don't understand . . . why pretend? Why let your teammates think that you don't support them?"

Ray's eyes dropped. "It's the way they look at me. They all feel sorry for me, and I can't stand that!" he said.

"So you act angry at them to put them off? To keep them from pitying you?"

"That's right. That way I can work on my grades without them always asking how it's going. Man, school is hard enough without people getting on your case all the time."

"And that's why you're at the library today?" she asked. "You're studying in order to push your grades up and get back on the team?"

He nodded. "Coach says that if I get my grade-point average up, he'll put me in the starting lineup next season."

Now Nancy understood. Ray wasn't handling his problems in the best possible way, in her opinion, but that wasn't her business. All that mattered to her was that he had no reason to hurt the Wildcats with practical jokes.

Of course, it was possible that he was lying to her, but the sincerity in his voice convinced Nancy that for once he was telling the truth.

She was glad, but nervous, too. With both Tom and Ray out of the running, she would now have to tell Ned something that she knew he didn't want to hear: His friend and co-captain, Mike O'Shea, was definitely responsible for the practical jokes—and a lot more, besides!

Chapter

Thirteen

THAT AFTERNOON AN enormous pep rally took
place in the gym. Emotions ran high as the band
played a medley of fight songs. The cheerleaders
whipped the crowd into a hand-clapping, foot-
stamping frenzy. The division championship was
at stake that night, and one question loomed large
in everyone's mind: Would the Wildcats win the
crown, or would they go down in defeat?

Nancy stood near the doors with Bess and
George, pondering a different question: When
and how would the practical joker strike next?
There was no doubt in her mind that he would. He
had to! This was his last chance to stop the team's
drive for the title.

As the rally's finale neared, a series of floats motored onto the court. A thousand purple and orange balloons fell from the ceiling as a platoon of baton twirlers kicked and smiled. It was an exciting scene, but Nancy was too worried to enjoy it.

A second later, George touched her arm. "Nancy, I think there's a problem outside. Want to check it out?"

Outside in the corridor, the team members were waiting to be introduced to the crowd. They were all nicely dressed in khaki slacks, ties, and Emerson, blazers, but on their faces were looks of worry. What now? Nancy wondered.

"Ned? What's going on?"

"It's Mike . . . he hasn't shown up yet," her boyfriend said tensely.

"He knew about the rally, right?"

"Of course he did!" Ned snapped irritably.

Nancy felt her face go red. Part of her wanted to shout at him, and part of her wanted to beg him not to be angry with her anymore. In the end, she did neither.

"Maybe he's been delayed for some reason," she suggested evenly.

Howie Little stepped forward and shook his head. "Mike's the first one to arrive anywhere, even for practice!"

"Yeah, it's not like him to go AWOL," Andy Hall added.

Nancy didn't see what she could do about the

situation. If her suspicions about Mike were correct—and she was certain that they were—there was no telling where he might be.

In the gym, the dean of the college stepped up to the microphone. *"And now it's time to meet our team!"* he announced. *"First, playing forward, number thirty-two . . . Kyle . . . Jefferson!"*

Cheers shook the gym. He was starting at the bottom of the roster, Nancy realized. That was good. It meant that Mike and Ned, the co-captains, would be the last to be introduced. Mike had a few more minutes to show.

One by one, the players walked into the gym as their names and numbers were called. Nancy watched the front entrance of the building anxiously, but finally Ned was the only one left in the corridor. Mike wasn't going to appear.

"Looks like I'll have to cover for him," Ned muttered. "Where *is* he?"

Inside the gym, the dean's voice rose excitedly. *"And next, the finest point guard in the history of our school . . . co-captain of the team, number seven . . . Ned . . . Nickerson!"*

The roar that burst from the crowd was thunderous. Ned strode confidently into the gym, stopped, and raised his arms in a victory sign. The roar grew even louder. Nancy was proud that Ned was so popular, but at the same time she felt terrible. She knew how torn up he must feel. This was definitely a moment he would want to share with Mike!

Slipping back into the gym, Nancy watched Ned step forward to the microphone and smoothly apologize for Mike's absence. Wisely, he didn't dwell on it, but moved straight into his thank-you's to the team's supporters.

As he talked, Nancy felt another touch on her arm. It was Pat Burnett. Like his team, the coach was wearing khakis, a tie, and an Emerson blazer. He also wore an identical look of worry—worry that she knew was growing from more than his concern over the upcoming game.

"Well, this is it. Our last game. I don't suppose you've had any luck since we last talked?"

Nancy had phoned the coach several times to update him on the case. There had been little to report, though—until now. She wasn't looking forward to telling him about his star forward.

She swallowed. "Yes, I have. Coach Burnett, I'm sorry to have to be the one to tell you this, but . . . but . . ."

Go on, tell him! she said to herself. Somehow she couldn't do it. The problem was, she wasn't totally sure that she was right. True, the evidence against Mike was overwhelming, yet for all that she still had no idea *why* he was doing such horrible things. Why was he pulling the pranks? Why was he assaulting innocent students? And why did he have two thousand dollars in his locker?

The money! All at once, Nancy remembered Tom Stafford's charge. Was it true that illegal salaries were being paid? If so, it might shed some light on Mike's motives, she knew. With all the tact at her command, Nancy quietly put the issue to the coach. His jaw tightened.

"Absolutely not, young lady," he pronounced when she had finished. "No Emerson player has ever . . . or *will* ever . . . be paid a penny to play for this school. Not while I'm around!"

"Is it possible that someone else could have made such payments?" Nancy asked. "Someone on the admissions staff, maybe?"

"No way! If they were doing anything like that, believe me, I'd know!"

She believed him. What else could she do? The force and conviction of his words were enough to persuade a stone!

Suddenly Nancy felt as if twenty tons of lead had been lifted from her shoulders. The coach's words meant that Ned was honest—every bit as honest as she had always believed! What a relief! At the same time, however, the denial left open the question of the money in Mike's locker. Where had it come from, if not from the school?

There was no time left for speculation, she knew. Her time was up. The coach was waiting impatiently for her report.

"Well, Nancy? Can you tell me the name of the practical joker?" he asked.

She nodded. "Unfortunately I can. Mr. Burnett, I'm afraid he's—"

Nancy never finished her sentence. At that

moment, a security guard rushed through the door and ran up to the coach.

"Mr. Burnett? You'd better come with me, sir," the guard panted. "One of your players is hurt. He says his name is Mike O'Shea, and it looks like he fell off the roof!"

Chapter

Fourteen

IN THE MIDDLE of the gym, Ned was getting ready to introduce the coach. Pat Burnett was already gone, however, and Nancy was only two steps behind him. She hated to leave Ned in such an awkward spot, but what could she do? Finding out about Mike came first!

Mike was lying in the snow near the base of one of the building's side walls. Glancing up, Nancy estimated the drop at sixty feet or so. The snow below her feet was only a foot deep, so Mike's fall had not been cushioned. Her heart began to race.

How badly was he hurt? It was hard to tell. One

thing *was* clear. He was in agony. His face was twisted with pain, and his breath came in shallow gulps.

"Hang on, Mike. The guards are bringing the ambulance around from the parking lot," the coach told him.

Nancy remembered seeing the vehicle in front of the building before the rally. State law required one to be present at every large public and sporting event.

Mike cried out. Sweat began to bead on his forehead. "Coach . . . get . . . get . . ."

"Like I said, the ambulance is on the way," the coach repeated.

"No! Get . . . Nancy Drew!"

Startled, Nancy stepped forward and sank down next to him. "I'm here, Mike."

"N-nancy . . . I've got to . . . to tell you what happened!" he gasped.

"I'm listening. But, Mike, please take it easy! You're hurt!"

"I know. Got to . . . to get to a hospital," he echoed weakly. "Listen . . . the one you're looking for is . . . is . . ."

Nancy bit her lip. Talking was obviously draining his strength. He should stop, yet she wanted him to continue! He was about to say something important, she felt. Something vital to the case!

"Get away from him!" barked a commanding

voice suddenly. "Make room! Make room! We've got to get him on this stretcher!"

The ambulance had arrived, and with it was Ed Riggs, the team doctor Nancy had met the first day on campus.

"Hurry! Get that thing over here!" Dr. Riggs shouted to the ambulance crew. "And you . . . Miss Drew! What do you think you're doing? Get away from him this instant!"

"Sorry." Embarrassed, Nancy rose and backed away. Quickly the medics lifted Mike and wheeled him to the ambulance. A moment later it was speeding to the hospital, its siren wailing.

The small crowd of people nearby began to disperse. Pat Burnett and Dr. Riggs hurried to the doctor's car for the ride to the hospital. Nancy planned to follow them in her Mustang, but first she had to check something out.

Backing away from the building, she glanced up at the roofline. There was a tubular metal railing up there, she noticed. It was about three or four feet high. Had Mike fallen over it accidentally? No way. The logical explanation was a lot simpler— and a lot more disturbing.

Mike had been pushed!

At the hospital, Nancy found Bess, George, and most of the team members already there, as well as several fans and faculty members.

The outpouring of concern for Mike made her ashamed. Ned wasn't the only one who believed in him, she could see. Others admired and respected him, too. How could she have been so wrong?

She *had* been wrong, of course. Mike hadn't pushed himself off that roof. Someone else had. The practical joker? Maybe, maybe not. Whoever it was, he had tried to kill Mike in order to keep him from spilling what he knew. It was obvious now that Mike was involved in something far bigger than she had imagined.

But what was it? A conspiracy against the team? Against the whole college? There was no way to know, and that infuriated her. Some detective she was turning out to be!

A short while later, Jan Teller arrived. When Ned told her what had happened to Mike, the petite brunette sank onto a couch and burst into tears. A hush fell over the room.

Silently, Ned sat down next to her and put his arms around her.

For what seemed like hours, they waited for some word from the doctors. At one point, Ray Ungar came in and sat quietly with his former teammates, confirming Nancy's belief that his loyalty to the team was genuine. It was no compensation.

At another point, Nancy tried to comfort Ned. He was alone now on a sofa, hunched over, his head in his hands. Nancy sat next to him and lightly placed her hand on his shoulder.

"Ned, I—"

He shrugged her off. Daggers seemed to shoot from his eyes as he turned to her. "Forget it, Nancy. There isn't anything you can say."

"I know, but I still want you to know that I'm sorry. Mike is your friend."

"You finally noticed, huh? Well, congratulations," he spat.

"Ned, please don't be like this."

"Why not? You never believed in him. For all I know you may still think he's responsible for all those pranks."

"I—" Nancy hesitated, uncertain of what to say. "Well, I do think one thing," she said finally. "This case isn't over yet. Not by a long shot."

"Brilliant, Nancy. Absolutely brilliant. Anybody can see that!"

Ned's sarcasm stung, but she deserved it, Nancy supposed. If she had done her work better, then maybe they wouldn't all be sitting in this emergency room right now!

Finally, a white-coated doctor appeared. Heads turned toward him. Ned and Jan leapt up simultaneously and rushed over to the man. "How is he?" Ned asked.

"His condition is serious, but he's stable," the doctor announced.

"How badly is he hurt?"

"Mike has a broken leg and multiple back injuries. We believe there may be some subdural hemorrhage of the spinal cord as well."

"What does *that* mean? Will he be okay?"

"He'll probably recover well enough to walk again, if that's what you mean."

"Walk!" Ned gasped. "What about basketball? Mike was planning to turn pro!"

The doctor shook his head sadly. "I'm sorry, young man, but I'm afraid that's impossible now. Mike's basketball days are over."

Groans of horror and dismay filled the air. He had to be kidding. Mike was one of the finest young players in the nation!

No one felt worse about the news than Nancy. Leaning against a wall for support, she silently vowed to work twice as hard to conclude this case. Partly her resolve sprang from guilt over Mike's condition, and partly it sprang from a sudden realization.

Mike was the victim of an attempted murder! Not only that, it was possible that the culprit would try to kill again!

Chapter

Fifteen

THAT EVENING, NANCY and her friends watched the game from the stands. Nancy was tense. She was still expecting another practical joke, but by halftime it had not been played. Why was the joker waiting so long? she wondered. Was he saving his knockout blow for the last minute?

Emerson's opponent that night was its archrival, Barton College. Traditionally, the match was a close one, but tonight it was even closer since Emerson was playing without its star forward, Mike O'Shea. Ned was doing an outstanding job of keeping the team together, Nancy saw, but even so it was rough going. Try as they might, the Wildcats' lead never rose above five points. Usually it was less.

When the second half started, the Wildcats threw themselves into the game as never before. Barton countered with a relentless man-to-man defense, but it wasn't enough. Slowly Emerson's score climbed, and at last it stabilized at an eight-point advantage. For every two points Barton scored, Emerson scored a matching pair. Every successful Barton foul shot was followed by an Emerson bucket.

The fans cheered nonstop. Nancy had never heard such loud support in her life. The storm of applause reached its peak with ten minutes to go, as Howie Little ran a fast break down court and scored with a spectacular double-handed slam dunk. As Ned and Howie exchanged a high five, Nancy was positive that the noise would bring down the roof.

As the game neared its end, however, she began to see signs of tension in the Emerson players. Andy Hall and Craig Watson looked especially unhappy. During a short break in the action, the two held a midcourt conference that ended with Craig shoving Andy. Nancy heard him shout, "C'mon, man, get with it! It's gonna be a push!"

Puzzled, Nancy turned to George. "What does *push* mean?" she asked.

"Beats me. I've never heard that term before," George replied.

Nancy's curiosity vanished less than a minute later. Just after the Wildcats threw the ball into play following a Barton foul shot, an accident occurred. At least it *seemed* like an accident.

Ned was dribbling the ball up the court with one hand and signaling his teammates with the other. At midcourt he glanced toward his coach. At the same moment, Craig and Andy ran a scissors cut—Craig brushing by Ned in front, Andy brushing past him from behind. The next instant Ned was on the floor, writhing. He had fallen!

Nancy screamed. She couldn't help it. Ned was hurt! He might even be seriously injured! Leaping up, she rushed to the sideline. She wanted to run onto the court, but a pair of security guards grabbed her by the arms, stopping her.

It took a long time for Ned to get up. Once he did, he had to be helped off the court by Dr. Riggs and the team's manager. He was limping, Nancy saw. His teeth clenched together with every step. But in spite of that, he wasn't ready to quit.

". . . I'm okay, honest," she heard him say as he approached.

Dr. Riggs shook his head firmly. "Baloney. I'm not letting you back on this court until I've had that foot X-rayed."

"But the game! The team needs me out there!" he pleaded.

"No dice. You're injured, and if I let you keep playing I'm just begging for a lawsuit on my last day of work."

"But, Dr. Riggs—!"

"Forget it. You're out of the game, and that's all there is to it."

When Nancy returned to her seat she was trembling. She was also deeply confused. Sitting, she began to think feverishly. Her program twisted around and around in her hands.

"Nan, what's the matter?" Bess asked. "Ned's all right, isn't he?"

"Yes. It's not Ned that's bothering me. It's what happened just now."

"What about it? It was only an accident."

"I don't think so. I think Ned was deliberately taken down."

George turned toward her in surprise. "You mean Craig and Andy put him out of action on purpose? But how? Why?"

"I'm not sure how. It happened so fast I couldn't really see. As to why, I'm not sure about that, either. But I've got to figure it out!"

On the court, the game resumed. Around her, the fans continued their chants and cheers. Nancy heard none of it. Elbows on her knees, she desperately tried to make sense out of the senseless events of the last five days.

Why would Craig and Andy hurt a member of their own team? Who had pushed Mike off the sports complex's roof? Who had been driving the black Camaro when the bus's tire was shot, and why was he also beating up Emerson students?

The questions went on endlessly. Nancy looked

at them from every angle she could think of. Still none of it made sense. Frustration swelled inside her like a balloon. If she didn't solve this mystery —and soon—she felt like she would burst!

The game entered its final minutes. With Ned out of action, Emerson slowly lost its lead. Seven points . . . six points . . . four points . . . soon Barton would overtake them and pull ahead!

"We're getting killed!" Bess cried, glancing at the clock. "What a time for Ned to be benched!"

George nodded grimly. "You said it! I'll bet the other team is happy about it, though."

Suddenly Nancy sat up. "George! What was that you just said?"

"Didn't you hear? I said, I'll bet the other team is happy."

In one magical burst of insight, everything fell into place. Nancy grabbed her friend's arm. "George, that's it! You just gave me the answer!"

Chapter

Sixteen

C'MON, YOU GUYS! We've got to find a phone!"
Leaping up, Nancy began to push her way to the
aisle. Bess and George exchanged puzzled looks
but quickly rose to follow her.

The lobby outside the gym was empty. Everyone, including the security guards, was inside
watching the game. Nancy spotted a pay phone on
the opposite wall and ran for it, digging all her
change from her pocket as she did.

Please let him be home! she prayed silently as
she punched out a long-distance number. On the
other end, the phone began to ring. Please let him
be there! If he is, I promise that I'll never run my
credit card over its limit again!

Carson Drew's voice was calm and steady when he finally answered. "Hello?"

"Dad, thank goodness you're home! I really need to talk to you!"

"Nancy! What is it?" her father asked. "Are you all right?"

"I'm fine, Dad, but this case has been driving me crazy. You wouldn't believe how weird it's been."

"Knowing you and your nose for trouble, I think I would." He laughed.

Nancy laughed then, too. It was such a relief to talk to him!

"Listen, I think I've worked out most of the puzzle, but there are still a few blank spots," she said. "I need your help to fill them in. Have you got the time?"

"Of course! Fire away," he offered.

Rapidly Nancy sketched the basics of her theory. Her father grasped the situation immediately, and in no time was giving her exactly the information that she needed.

Nancy smiled. Most people knew that Carson Drew was a highly respected criminal lawyer, but few realized that in addition to defending the innocent he also defended the guilty. He knew a lot about crime. Now that knowledge proved highly useful. Her grin broadened as he finished.

"Thanks, Dad. That does it . . . oh, except for one thing. Does the term *push* mean anything special to you?"

It did. Nancy listened for a few seconds longer, then said a hasty goodbye. Hanging up, she turned to Bess and George.

"Okay, let's roll!"

"Wait a minute! What's going on, Nancy?" George demanded.

"Yeah," Bess echoed. "Aren't you going to fill us in?"

"There isn't time. The culprit is probably getting ready to escape right this minute. We've got to stop him!"

Nancy paused to check one final fact, however. Opening the directory that hung on a chain below the pay phone, she looked up a number: the number on the scrap of paper she'd picked up in the bookstore phone booth. Then, satisfied, she started down the main corridor, away from the gym. She motioned for her friends to follow her, then zipped down a stairway.

As they walked, the sounds of the game faded behind them. The final buzzer must be near, Nancy knew, but they would have to wait to find out who won. There wasn't a second to lose!

The final corridor to which they came was just as Nancy remembered it. Like the first time she had gone down it, it was silent. The noise from the gym was no more than a memory here. Stopping at a familiar door, she whispered to her friends.

"You guys are my backup. If things get out of hand in there"—she pointed to the door—"I'll scream my head off."

"But, Nancy, who's inside?" Bess hissed.

"You'll see. Remember, listen for my scream . . . if you hear it, run for the police!"

This was it. If everything went as she hoped, the case would be wrapped up in a matter of minutes! Nancy took a deep breath. Stepping up to the door, she opened it without knocking, slipped around it, and closed it behind her.

Dr. Riggs was standing behind his desk, stuffing files and notebooks into a gym bag. As she came in, his head snapped up.

"What the—"

"Hello, Doctor," she said with a smile.

"Nancy Drew! What do *you* want?"

"I want to congratulate you on the success of your gambling ring," she said. "Tell me, Doctor . . . how does it feel to retire rich?"

Chapter

Seventeen

SILENCE FELL. DR. Riggs said nothing. Instead he stared at her for a full minute. He didn't even blink. She had to give him one thing, Nancy decided: He was cool. Very cool.

Finally, the doctor returned to his files and notebooks. One by one he placed them in the gym bag. His movements were slow and deliberate. He was buying time, she knew.

"Well, Miss Drew," he said at last. "That's an interesting accusation. I'm running a gambling ring, you say?"

"From this very office. If I were you I'd go to the police right now and make a full confession," she said.

"Why should I do that?"

"Because they'll go easier on you if you turn yourself in voluntarily."

"Really!" He shook his head in amusement. "That's fascinating."

Suddenly Nancy's patience gave out. "Come on, Doctor . . . stop pretending. You're guilty and we both know it!"

"Do we?" His face grew hard. "All I've heard so far is wild fantasies from a would-be detective, Miss Drew."

"You want proof?"

"If you have any. Frankly, though, I think you're nothing more than a teenager with an overactive imagination."

An overactive—! Nancy was furious. Had she imagined the black Camaro? The list in Mike's locker? Her near-death in the sauna? No way! She crossed her arms.

"I should have realized what was going on my second day on campus," she began. "I overheard a student called Captain Hook asking for a ten-timer. That's a fifty-dollar bet, but I didn't know that at the time."

Dr. Riggs continued to pack his gym bag, but his eyes never left her.

"Strangely enough, I ran across Captain Hook again," Nancy went on. "This time he was out cold. He had been beaten up because he couldn't pay off his gambling losses. Even then I still didn't guess the truth. I was too busy hunting for the practical joker."

"Ah, yes! The practical joker! Is that me, too, Miss Drew?"

"No. I'm getting to that. First I want to explain how the gambling worked . . . call it practice for what I'm going to tell the police."

"Go on."

"A few days before each Wildcat game you set a 'line,' Dr. Riggs. That's a point spread between the winning and losing teams. Those who bet on the correct side of the line won the amount they wagered. Those who bet on the wrong side of the line paid the amount of their wager, plus a ten-percent 'vig.'"

"Vig?"

"That's short for vigorish, your commission on the losing bet."

"I see. Please continue."

"Well, it was a nice scam. You made a lot of money. But you weren't satisfied, Dr. Riggs. You wanted more, so eventually you began to set the line low. That made people bet *above* it, since they knew Emerson would whip their opponents by a bigger margin than the line indicated."

Nancy paused. Dr. Riggs was no longer packing his gym bag.

"After that," she went on, "all you had to do was make sure that the final scores fell below the line. You did that with the help of certain Emerson players . . . scholarship students like Mike O'Shea, Andy Hall, and Craig Watson. They shaved points in the final minutes of the games, and the result was lots of extra vig."

"Oh?"

"Yes, and you shared that money with them in the form of watches, clothes . . . even cash. Mike has two thousand dollars in small bills hidden inside his locker."

"That's all very well, Miss Drew, but you still haven't explained the practical jokes . . . where do they fit in?"

"Oh, those . . . they were staged by the players themselves to account for their jitters—and the shaved points."

All at once the atmosphere in the room grew menacing. Dr. Riggs regarded her coldly, his mouth set in a tight line.

"Well, well . . . how did you manage to figure out all that?"

"I had a little help," Nancy confessed, sending a mental thank-you to her father. "I'm not finished, though, Doctor. I still need to tell you who shot out the bus's tire and who pushed Mike off the roof and—"

"Don't bother. You've already said quite enough, I think."

Reaching into the top drawer of his desk, the doctor drew out a large revolver. He pointed it at her heart.

"You're very clever, Nancy Drew. But not clever enough!"

"P-put that down!" Nancy stammered weakly. "Put it down or I'll scream."

"You do, and it will be the last sound that ever leaves your mouth."

He wasn't kidding, she could see. He really would shoot her! The barrel of the revolver wasn't wavering in the slightest!

"Now, Miss Drew, it's my turn to talk," he said. "I'm going to give you some instructions, and I want you to follow them to the letter. Do you understand?"

Nancy nodded.

"First, walk slowly up to my desk and pick up that pen . . . fine. See that scrap of paper? Yes, that one! I want you to write the following message on it."

Startled, she looked up at him.

"Oh, come now . . . don't look so surprised! I know you must have your two friends waiting outside. Here's the message: False alarm. Go to the student union and wait for me there. Will explain later."

Nancy wrote the words exactly as he had dictated them. She was signing her death certificate, she knew, but what else could she do?

"Finished? Let me see. Now fold the paper and take two steps backward. Excellent. Don't move."

Dr. Riggs walked around his desk to stand next

to Nancy. "Move slowly toward the door. I want you to open it just a bit very, very carefully and pass the note to your friends. Don't say a word. Then shut the door. And remember, I'll be right behind you."

Nancy did as she was told. "Now step back and turn around," Dr. Riggs commanded. "Place your hands on top of your head."

His gun still trained on her, Dr. Riggs moved back behind his desk. Next he reached for his telephone. A minute later, his call completed, he replaced the receiver.

"All right, Miss Drew. . . . Now we wait."

For what seemed like an eternity, they stayed as they were: Nancy with her hands on her head, Dr. Riggs with the gun pointing at her heart. Desperately, Nancy tried to think of a way out, but no plan came to her. The gun had her spellbound.

Finally, she couldn't stand the tension any longer. "What are you going to do with me?" she whispered. "Lock me in the sauna again?"

Dr. Riggs smiled. "Ah! So you know I was the one who did that!"

"Of course. I had to slip past your office that night. You saw me, I guess, and followed me to the locker room."

"Correct. Too bad you managed to escape that time. Now I've got to find another way of killing you."

Just then, Nancy heard the door behind her open. It closed again quickly.

"You're here!" Dr. Riggs beamed. "About time. Grab her."

A powerful pair of hands seized her from behind. Nancy struggled, but it was no use. In seconds her arms were pinned to her sides.

She had already guessed what was coming next. Dr. Riggs went to his medicine cabinet and soaked a handkerchief with chloroform. When he applied it to her mouth and nose, she was surprised at how much it stung—her throat felt like it was on fire!

"That's it . . . breathe deeply. It's quicker that way!"

Slowly, time began to distort. Nancy felt her struggling grow weaker, her eyelids grow heavy. It was like sinking backward into a pool, she decided . . . a deep, black pool. . . .

Chapter

Eighteen

WHEN NANCY CAME to she was still in Dr. Riggs's office. Dr. Riggs was missing, but the guy who had seized her from behind was not. As she brought him into focus, blinking, he smiled. He was holding the revolver.

"Feeling better?" he asked. His voice was like sandpaper, and his tall, thin frame looked whipcord strong.

Nancy didn't answer. She was afraid that if she tried to speak, she would be sick. She closed her eyes again.

"Not feeling too talkative, I guess. Can't say that I blame you."

For a minute, nothing happened. Nancy simply

let the fog of semiconsciousness drift through her mind. What was happening? Where was Ned? They were supposed to be going out on a date tonight, weren't they? The movies, maybe, or—

No!

The truth, when it hit, was sharp as an electric shock. This was no date. This was a very dangerous situation. She was in the hands of criminals. She was probably going to die!

Little by little, she forced herself to wake up. Opening her eyes, she took stock. Her location? She was lying on the examination table: *bad*. The guy with the gun? He was leaning against the desk, watching her: *also bad*. Bess and George? Oh, yes, they were on a wild goose chase in the student union . . .

. . . very, very bad!

It all added up to not very much in her favor. Groggily, she sat up and swiveled around so that she was perched on the edge of the examination table. Yes, that was better.

"You're Frank, aren't you?" she said.

The guy looked startled. "How did you know my name?"

"I heard Captain Hook use it on the phone," she explained.

"Oh, him. Stupid jerk. He shouldn't have used it to help him make his bet. Just got himself into trouble in the end."

Some trouble! He had been beaten until he was unconscious!

"Where's Dr. Riggs?" Nancy asked next.

Frank said nothing.

"Don't bother, I think I know," she continued. "He's at the hospital finishing the job on Mike—the job you started to do this afternoon on the roof!"

"Don't know how he survived that fall," Frank said, shaking his head in puzzlement. "I was sure it would kill him!"

That confirmed it. Now Nancy was positive about the "important business" Mike had wanted to take care of that morning—he had tried to tell Dr. Riggs that he was backing out of the point-shaving scam, and Dr. Riggs had ordered Frank to shut Mike up—permanently!

Nancy was also positive of something else: Frank had been instructed to do the same to her! As soon as she could walk, no doubt, Frank would take her to his black Camaro and drive her away. Then he would dispose of her.

But would he really do it? Nancy thought about it and decided that he would. After all, he had a big stake in the gambling operation: He was the one who picked up payments, dropped off winnings, and punished those who couldn't cover their losses. Dr. Riggs was probably giving him a major share of the loot.

She had to stall, she knew. She needed time to think of a plan!

"How is Dr. Riggs going to get rid of Mike?" she asked.

Frank eyed her suspiciously. "Now why would a nice girl like you want to know something like that?" he demanded.

"I . . . uh . . . just curious, that's all."

"Well, I suppose I can tell you, seeing as you won't be around to repeat it. Riggs said Mike would die of an embolism."

Air injected into the bloodstream! Nancy winced. How horrible. Once the bubbles got into Mike's heart, he would die within minutes. Was there any chance she could save him, too?

She continued to stall. "And how did you get involved with Dr. Riggs?" she asked.

"Nosy, aren't you? Riggs recruited me from the county hospital."

"What did you do there?"

"I was a male nurse. Funny, huh? Before, I made people feel better. Now I make them feel worse!" He chuckled at the witticism.

Nancy was revolted.

"Hey, don't look so uptight. If Riggs promised you as much money as he promised me, you'd be working for him, too."

"I doubt that." Nancy was getting impatient. She had to get free soon—but how?.

Frank seemed to sense the new urgency she was feeling. "You're looking awfully perky," he said. "I think it's time to take you for a nice, long ride, Nancy Drew."

Bending over, he reached for a piece of rope that was lying by his feet. Nancy saw her chance.

Bracing herself with her hands, she pushed herself off the examination table and at the same time kicked upward with her foot.

The kick wasn't strong enough to knock Frank out, but it did catch him squarely in the face. Howling, he fell backward onto the desk. Blood gushed from his shattered nose, but Nancy didn't hang around to see more. Heart pounding, she ran to the door and opened it.

Running was difficult. Nancy was still groggy from the chloroform. She felt herself weaving back and forth, pushing off walls, tripping and getting up. No matter what, though, she kept going. She would only get one chance!

How long had she delayed Frank with that kick? Not very long, she was sure. He was probably after her already. He had the revolver, too. Somehow she had to get out of the building—she'd have a better chance in the open. A car might come by. Someone might hear her scream.

On and on she ran. Why had they made the halls so long? Finally, she reached a stairway and staggered up it. Another long hall and she was in the main lobby.

It was empty, of course. The game was long over, and everyone had gone home. Even the security guard wasn't around. Anxiously, she raced to the glass front doors and pushed. They were locked! She glanced around wildly for another way out—and spotted it. Off to her right, another set of doors!

Sprinting, she burst through them—and stopped dead. She was in the gym! This wasn't any good—she was a sitting duck in the middle of all this space.

What next?

Nancy was almost ready to give up when she spotted the floats. Ever since the pep rally that afternoon two of them had been parked on one side of the gym, next to some bleachers. She ran for the nearest one as fast as she could.

The float was a high platform, below which hung a pleated curtain. Ducking under this, she saw that the whole thing rested on the roof of a Jeep! What luck! If she could only get it started, then maybe, just maybe—

Footsteps sounded on the wooden floor outside. Frank was in the gym, stalking her. Quietly, Nancy slipped into the Jeep's driver's seat and reached for the key. It wasn't there. She would have to hot-wire it, she realized, but how could she do that without giving herself away? One sound and she was dead!

Reaching under the dashboard, she located the ignition wires. She tugged them down and began to twist them together. How did it go? The red and the white? The black and the green? If she got out of this alive, she promised herself, she would practice stealing cars until she could do it blind-folded!

The engine caught. Nancy stomped on the gas pedal, slammed the gearshift into first, and popped the clutch. The float jerked forward. She was in motion! Now she had just one more problem to solve: Where to go?

Nancy flicked on the headlights. As she did, she saw that a rectangle had been cut out of the curtain in front of the windshield. The view wasn't great, but it would have to do. She headed for the middle of the court.

Where was Frank? Nancy couldn't see him, but she knew he was there. It wouldn't be long before he started shooting, either. Her only hope lay in being difficult to hit. On that theory, she began to drive in circles, looking both for Frank and a possible way out.

There! She had it! On the other side of the gym was a long row of double doors—the exit to the parking lot. Spinning the wheel, she headed for them—then hit the brakes. Twenty yards ahead of her, Frank had stepped from the darkness into the glare of the headlights!

Slowly, Frank raised the revolver and squeezed off a shot. The windshield shattered. Nancy screamed and covered her face with her hands. She was trapped!

Chapter

Nineteen

WHAT WAS SHE going to do? There was no hope. Unless . . .

Pushing in the clutch, she slammed the gearshift into first again. The Jeep began to roll. She was heading directly at Frank, but he didn't move. Instead, he squeezed off two more shots. Nancy hit the horn and accelerated. Why didn't he jump out of the way? Why didn't he—

At the last moment, he twisted sideways and dove. Pressing down the accelerator, Nancy headed straight for the exit doors. When she reached them she didn't stop—she plowed straight through.

The Jeep died in the parking lot. Nancy felt as if

she was going to die, too. Every bone in her body ached. She felt like she had just driven through a brick wall.

"Look! Over there!"

George! Wrenching open the door, Nancy fought her way out of the now-ruined float. Across the parking lot she saw her friend running toward her—and with her were Bess, Ned, and at least a dozen policemen.

She was safe!

An hour later, Nancy was sitting in Pat Burnett's office. She had just given the coach her final report, and now Bess and George were falling over each other in their eagerness to tell their part of the story. Nancy grinned as she listened.

". . . so after waiting in the student union for an hour, we realized that something was wrong. We went to the hospital, figuring we'd find Ned there. That's when we saw Dr. Riggs. We asked him—"

"—if he'd seen you, but his answer sounded fishy. So we followed him to Mike's room. Just then Ned walked by . . . he was talking to a doctor . . . and we filled him in. The doctor was suspicious, too, so we ran into Mike's room, and sure enough! Dr. Riggs—"

"—was getting ready to inject a syringe full of *air* into Mike's arm! Can you believe that? What a creep!"

"Yeah. Well, to make a long story short, we had

him arrested. Then we rushed over here to the sports complex."

"We arrived just in time to see you drive that float out the side entrance. Boy, did *that* look weird!"

"I'll bet it did," Nancy said.

Behind his desk, Pat Burnett grunted and leaned back in his chair. "I owe you an apology, young lady," he announced. "If I had known how much danger was involved, I never would have called you in to investigate this case."

Nancy shook her head. "Don't apologize. You had no idea what was going on."

"I certainly didn't. And I'm still not too clear about one thing . . . how did you know that Riggs was behind it all?"

"Remember the warning spray painted on the window of our dorm room? That happened the first night. At the time, only three people besides Bess and George knew that I was investigating the practical jokes: you, Ned . . . and Dr. Riggs! I should have seen the significance of it sooner, but I didn't."

"There's something else you haven't told us, Nancy," Bess put in. "What's a *push?*"

Nancy explained, "Craig and Andy were worried that the final point spread would be eight—exactly on the line for tonight. If that happened it would be a push. All bets would be off, and nobody would collect any vig."

"Is that why they knocked Ned down? To keep him from pushing the score over the line?"

"That's right."

George looked over. "I have a question, too. What made you realize that gambling was involved, Nancy?"

"Oh! It was the comment you made after Ned was taken down. You said, 'I'll bet the other team is happy.' Remember?"

"Yes, but—"

"It was the word *bet* that hit me. I put it together with Captain Hook's phone call, and voilà! Everything fell into place."

Silence descended in the office. As Nancy relaxed, letting the tension finally drain out of her system, she suddenly realized that there was something *she* didn't know.

"Coach Burnett, in all the excitement I forgot to ask. Who won the game?"

"We did, by two points," he said.

There was no joy in his voice. No doubt he was thinking about the NCAA playoffs, she knew. The Wildcats weren't going to have much of a chance with their best players out of commission. She felt bad for him.

What a lot of trouble had come out of a few practical jokes!

Ned was waiting for her in the lobby. Without a word, they went out the front doors together and began to wander slowly across the campus. The moon cast blue shadows around them. Nancy felt as if she were walking the last mile.

"Ned, you can forgive me for suspecting Mike, can't you?" she asked.

Ned shook his head. "I don't know, Nancy. I just don't know . . ."

"But he was involved in the point shaving. He made that effigy, too. You accept that, don't you?"

"Yes. What I can't accept is the way you handled everything. If you hadn't confronted him the way you did . . . if you had been more understanding . . . then maybe . . ."

"What?"

"Well, he might have opened up to you. Or to me. Instead he tried to handle everything himself, and look what happened! He's flat on his back in the hospital. He'll never play basketball again!"

There was nothing Nancy could say to that. Ned was right. Because she had been angry at him, she had tried to prove him wrong. She had charged ahead without any thought about the consequences.

She could see now that Mike O'Shea wasn't a bad person. He was simply a vulnerable guy from a poor background who had been offered some easy money. He had listened to his conscience, too, and had tried to break free. But had she taken that possibility into consideration? No, she had not. She had tagged Mike as a criminal.

What had gone wrong? How had she managed to lose her usual good judgment? It had been a stressful case, of course, but that didn't excuse her. The greater the pressure, she knew, the more important it was for her to stay loose.

Maybe it was something else, she thought. Maybe being a detective was making it difficult for her to trust people. After all, look at her and Ned! In spite of their relationship, she had even suspected *him* for a while!

Remembering the bracelet he had given her, Nancy asked a question that had been on her mind since early that evening.

"Ned, where did you get the money for that silver bracelet?"

He shrugged. "Where else? It came out of the money I earned lifeguarding last summer."

"Oh. Then why did you keep it a secret? When I said something about the price that night at the party, you brushed me off."

Ned walked in silence for a minute, his eyes on the stars. When he finally answered her, his voice was remote.

"Nancy, do you realize how hard it is for me to give you anything?"

"What do you mean? Ned, you've given me lots of things! Balloons, chocolates—"

"I'm not talking about gifts. I'm talking about more important things . . . love, support, sympathy . . . that stuff."

"Ned, are you nuts?" she cried. "You're the most loving, generous guy in the world!"

"And you're the most independent girl in the world, too. Nancy, you don't need me. There's nothing I give you that you can't get from a hundred other guys."

"Ned!"

"It's true. Not only that, when you get right down to it, who comes first in our relationship? You! Your career! Your cases! Even your suspects!"

"But—"

"Every time I help you with a case, you keep me in the background. My opinion means nothing to you! Well, let me tell you something . . . I'm sick of being put down and ignored. Nancy, I can't even give you a bracelet without hearing you ask how much money I spent on it!"

Nancy was stunned. Never before had she heard him sound so angry, so bitter. Had she really been acting as horribly as he said? Had she really been treating him so badly?

Stopping, she turned and touched his arm. "Ned, what are you saying? I don't understand why you're so upset. I mean, we've shared everything . . . the danger, the fun. . . ."

"Sure, but that's not what I want anymore. It's not enough."

"What do you mean?"

He ran his fingers through his hair. "Nancy, I've

been thinking about it for the last few days, and . . . well, I think it's time for us to start seeing other people."

The words hit Nancy like a slap. "N-Ned . . . you don't mean that—"

"Yes, I do. I can't live with the way things are between us any longer. You're changing, Nancy. You don't trust people anymore . . . not even me."

"That's not true!"

"Then what about Mike? When I told you he was okay, why didn't you believe me?"

Once again there was nothing she could say. She hadn't believed him. But did she have to pay for it by losing Ned?

"Ned, I love you," she whispered. "Please don't leave me."

"I'm sorry, Nancy. My mind's made up. We can still be friends, I guess. Or at least we can try to be."

"Ned, no!"

"Goodbye, Nancy. And good luck on your next case, whatever it is."

With that, he turned and walked away. Nancy watched him disappear down a snowy path, her mouth hanging open. This couldn't be happening! How could they be breaking up after all this time?

A minute later, he was out of sight. He didn't come back, either. Nancy desperately wanted to see his face one more time, to plead with him to change his mind. But she wasn't going to get that chance, she knew. It was over. For good.

Turning away, Nancy walked off into the darkness. In the distance, a siren began to wail. A vast emptiness opened inside her, and for the first time that she could remember, she began to cry.

Nancy's next case:

It was hard enough breaking up with Ned. Now he's come back—not to make up, but to ask Nancy to help his new girlfriend!

A priceless diamond disappears in the middle of a ballet, and young dancer Belinda Morrison is accused of the daring onstage robbery.

Nancy and her new boyfriend, Brad Eastman, investigate the crime. But as they dig deeper, they find the job getting harder—and ever more dangerous.

Just how dangerous? Find out in *FALSE MOVES*, Case #9 in The Nancy Drew Files.